D0911230

HIDING OUT

Toronto Public Library
Sanderson

JAN - 2018

Visit us at www.boldstrokesbooks.com

HIDING OUT

by
Kay Bigelow

2017

HIDING OUT

© 2017 BY KAY BIGELOW. ALL RIGHTS RESERVED.

ISBN 13: 978-1-62639-983-9

THIS TRADE PAPERBACK ORIGINAL IS PUBLISHED BY
BOLD STROKES BOOKS, INC.
P.O. BOX 249
VALLEY FALLS, NY 12185

FIRST EDITION: OCTOBER 2017

THIS IS A WORK OF FICTION. NAMES, CHARACTERS, PLACES, AND INCIDENTS ARE THE PRODUCT OF THE AUTHOR'S IMAGINATION OR ARE USED FICTITIOUSLY. ANY RESEMBLANCE TO ACTUAL PERSONS, LIVING OR DEAD, BUSINESS ESTABLISHMENTS, EVENTS, OR LOCALES IS ENTIRELY COINCIDENTAL.

THIS BOOK, OR PARTS THEREOF, MAY NOT BE REPRODUCED IN ANY FORM WITHOUT PERMISSION.

CREDITS
EDITOR: KATIA NOYES
PRODUCTION DESIGN: STACIA SEAMAN
COVER DESIGN BY MELODY POND

Acknowledgments

I want to thank my fellow authors and the staff of Bold Strokes Books for answering my numerous questions thoroughly and with patience. I would also like to thank my editor, Katia Noyes, for her patience as we moved through the manuscript.

For Reddeer—for her love and support

CHAPTER ONE

Treat didn't know what to do with herself. Brattleboro, Vermont, didn't offer much in the way of daytime diversions. The afternoon before, she'd explored the entire town. There were several bookstores, but she wasn't really in the mood to browse books. She didn't need to buy anything, and there was little in the way of shopping unless you wanted to purchase a bicycle or sporting clothes. Rather than hole up in her room at the Latchis Hotel with its view of the parking lot, Treat decided to check on the status of the home she was having built in a nearby town. Her house was nearing completion, and she needed to do a walk-through before the builder let the building inspector inside for final approvals. She'd arrived prepared to do the inspection only to be told it would be a few more days before that could happen.

While her property was only fifteen minutes from downtown Brattleboro, it felt like it was in another world. Treat drove to her property using the map she'd used six years earlier during a spring trip, and the beauty of the surrounding hills awed her again. Late spring in Vermont had been spectacular, with daffodils and crocuses running amok everywhere. One of the owners of a downtown bookstore had told her then it was the best time of year because people were coming out of hibernation. It was, in fact, the reason she and Chloe had purchased the property.

Today, in late September, she drove slowly with her windows down, savoring the still-warm weather, the rolling hills nearby, and the lack of traffic. The trees were thinking about turning colors, and every once in a while, there'd be a tree ahead of its time, already in its bright orange or crimson glory.

She turned onto her newly paved driveway and stopped. She left her car and stood with her eyes closed and her face raised to the warmth of the sun. As she stood listening, all she could hear was silence. After spending twenty years in California where there was always noise of one sort or another, traffic on freeways and streets, the occasional gunshot, barking dogs, or the raised voices of adults and children, the quiet of the countryside was disconcerting. Slowly, as if trusting she was no threat, birds began to sing. In the distance, she heard the rat-a-tat-tat of what she thought might be a woodpecker. All around her, the gently undulating hills were still mostly green. When a slight breeze came up she watched it as it moved across the meadow, the still grass moving gracefully as a gentle breeze passed by. When the breeze caressed her, Treat smelled the earth. *If this is what peace is, I want more of it.*

Both the silence and her reverie were interrupted by the ringing of her cell phone. Her attorney wanted her to know the town could do the final inspection on Tuesday, so she would need to do a walk-through with the builder no later than Monday. As much as she wanted to stay where she was and enjoy the view and the peace, she also wanted to see, and feel, her new home more.

Treat drove up the long driveway and stopped as it began curving past the house. There were several vehicles scattered about, providing physical proof the construction crew was busy finishing her home. She was pleased to see the builder had been able to keep the huge maple near her front door with no apparent damage to the tree. She let her eyes roam over the front of her two-story house. It was exactly as she and Chloe had pictured it on the night they designed it. She glanced to her right to the area where the landscaper had said would be a flower garden the following spring, and literally did a double take.

"Dear God," she whispered.

In the middle of her yet-to-be flower garden, a woman was working. She was tall, muscled, and tanned. Her short hair was a striking auburn.

"Can I help you?" a male voice asked, startling Treat from her contemplation of the woman.

Treat couldn't tell whether her heart was beating wildly because of the woman she was watching or at being surprised by the male voice so close to her. When her heart slowed its wild flight, she said, "I'm Treat Dandridge."

"You the owner of this place, then?"

"That would be me."

"I'll get Sloan for you."

Treat stayed where she was as her attention was drawn back to the woman working in her garden. She was hand-sanding a long plank of wood, and with each stroke, Treat could see the muscles of her arms and legs tense as she was forced to stretch to reach the end of the wood. She continued to sand the wood in easy fluid movements, stroke after stroke. Treat was mesmerized by those long strokes.

❖

The object of Treat's fascination, Mickey Heiden, heard a car come up the driveway but paid no attention to it since cars came and went throughout the day. When she felt someone watching her, however, the fine hairs on the back of her neck stood up, and a spike of fear ran down her spine. *It's probably nothing other than me being overly cautious. Or paranoid.* At least she hoped that was all it was.

❖

Sloan arrived, breaking Treat's concentration and forcing her to stop staring at the carpenter. Treat stepped out of her car to greet him.

"Ms. Dandridge. What can I do for you?" Sloan wanted to know.

Treat resisted the impulse to say he could introduce her to the woman she'd been staring at. Instead, she said, "My attorney informed me I need to do the final walk-through this weekend. I had a couple of free hours this morning and wanted to see the progress. I hope you don't mind the intrusion."

Sloan laughed. "No, I don't. The fact you only come when called is both a miracle and much appreciated."

"I won't stay long. A quick look and then I'll be gone."

Treat stole another glance at the woman. Sloan caught her looking.

"She's one of our carpenters. She's building the last bookcase for your office. Come on, I'll give you the grand tour."

He led the way toward the front door.

"Your home is, for all practical purposes, ready for you to move in," Sloan said as they entered the foyer. "If you like what you see today, I'll call the building inspector. He has an opening on Tuesday. Once he signs off on the house, it will be yours, and you can move in. The last thing done is the landscaping, but you can live here while they finish their job."

Sloan led her up the staircase to the right of the front door and through every room. They finished in the living room. When Sloan's phone rang, he said, "Excuse me, I need to get this."

Treat opened the French doors and stepped outside onto the brick patio. From there, she could see the carpenter to her right. She decided to introduce herself and started toward her. The woman straightened up and slowly turned toward Treat.

Treat had to tell herself to breathe as the woman stood studying her, her eyes roaming slowly down Treat's body. She resisted the temptation to run her hand through her hair, pull on her shirt to make sure it was straight, and check to make sure her zipper was up. Treat, who hadn't been self-conscious since she was fifteen, was now wondering what the woman saw. When the woman's eyes returned to meet hers, she elevated an auburn eyebrow. Treat was aware the woman exuded sex, and she was not immune to its allure.

❖

Mickey watched the woman approach. She was slender and an inch or two short of six feet. She exuded power, wealth, and something else Mickey couldn't quite put her finger on. She looked like she belonged in Manhattan or Paris, not Guilford, Vermont, population 2,100. *What would cause a woman like this to want to live in rural Vermont?*

❖

When Treat dared to look at the woman again, there was a slight smile on her lips. *What is she finding so damned amusing?*

As Treat closed the distance between them, she was

surprised at the unusual color of her eyes. They were gray—the gray of a stormy day. Treat held out her hand as she reached the woman.

"I wanted you to know how much I admire the work you've done inside."

"Thank you."

The woman's cheeks were slightly pink. *Is that a blush? I can't remember the last time I saw a grown woman blush. Surely the woman has received a compliment before.*

"I'm Treat Dandridge. This is my home."

"I certainly hope so, or else Sloan is letting strangers wander about someone else's property."

Treat heard a wisp of Southern drawl in the woman's voice. She'd always been a sucker for women with a hint of the South in their voices.

"Yeah, I guess that's obvious."

"My name is Mickey. Mickey Heiden."

"Nice name." *Nice name? Good God, Treat, can you sound any more banal?*

"Yeah. I kinda like it, and it fit into the neighborhood in Boston."

"Is that where you're from?"

"Nope."

Oh good, one of those Yankees whose idea of a conversation is "yep" and "nope."

"Well, it was good to meet you. Perhaps I'll see you again on my next trip out here."

"Probably not. My work here will be completed this weekend."

If Treat wanted to see this woman again, she better ask her right now. *Do you really want to see her again? No. Yes. No.* She could imagine having an excruciating dinner trying to get her dinner companion to say something besides short sentences and yep and nope. *No, the woman is drop-dead gorgeous, but not worth the effort of maintaining a one-sided conversation.* Treat, however, knew she was lying to herself.

"I appreciate your work here," Treat told her again and turned away to find Sloan and finish her business here.

❖

Mickey didn't want Treat to go. Treat was, simply put, the stuff dreams are made of, tall, dark, and mysterious. As much as she wasn't interested in having only one woman, she knew Treat might be able to change her mind about being single. Mickey had known they were building this house for a woman, but she'd not imagined it would be one who looked like she could have stepped out of someone's wet dream. If she didn't say something soon, Treat would walk back into the house and out of her life.

❖

"Would you like to have dinner with me tonight?" Mickey asked in a graceless rush.

Treat stopped dead in her tracks. She turned slowly back to Mickey, unsure whether it had been Mickey who had spoken or wishful thinking on her part.

"I'd love to have dinner with you."

Treat wasn't sure which of them was the more surprised at her response.

Treat broke the lengthening silence first. "Perhaps you'd like to tell me where we'll be having dinner?"

Treat smiled when Mickey blushed again.

"Sure," Mickey said, trying to sound casual. "It will be at my house. I can grill steaks and fresh asparagus for us, if that's okay?"

"It would be wonderful."

Treat watched as Mickey reached beneath her sawhorses and pulled a triangular-shaped piece of wood from a small pile of cast-offs. She dug a carpenter's pencil from a pocket and wrote her name and cell number on the wood. She even drew a crude map of how to get to her house from the Latchis Hotel. Treat wondered how Mickey knew she was staying at the Latchis when she remembered it was the only hotel in town. Mickey handed the piece of wood to Treat.

"Thanks."

When Mickey didn't say anything, Treat asked, "Time?"

"Can you make it around six?" Mickey asked.

"I can. Can I bring something? Wine, perhaps?"

"I don't drink alcohol, so bring whatever you'd like to drink. But you don't need to bring anything."

"I'll think of something. See you later."

"I certainly hope so," Mickey said so softly that, again, Treat wasn't sure whether Mickey had actually said it out loud or if it was her own words inside her head she'd heard. She was, however, acutely aware Mickey was watching her walk away. *Do not look back, Treat.*

When she returned to the living room, Sloan was waiting for her. He asked, "Well? Should I call the inspector?"

"By all means."

The house was exactly as she and Chloe had envisioned their dream home to be. She already felt at home even though there wasn't a stick of furniture in the house. She knew this was where she needed to be.

Sloan asked her to sign a document saying she approved

the house as he had shown it to her. She gladly signed her approval. He led her back to the front door.

"What do you really think?" he asked as he held out his hand.

"I love it. It's everything I asked for," Treat said, shaking his hand. "Thanks for showing me around."

As she opened the car door, she paused and leaned against the car watching Mickey. She was again sanding boards and didn't turn around. Treat wondered how long she could observe. She was being silly, she knew. She'd see Mickey again in a few hours. She got in the car and, with one last glance at the carpenter, drove toward the road leading back to Brattleboro. She couldn't resist looking in the rearview mirror and laughed when she saw Mickey watching her drive away. She was disappointed to find herself at the end of the driveway and no longer able to see the other woman.

Mickey hadn't behaved that stupidly with a girl since her first girlfriend in eighth grade. *I'm a trial attorney, for God's sake. I don't get tongue-tied*, she reminded herself. And the voice of pure reason in the back of her head responded with *Ah, but you did with this one. Whatever does it mean?* It doesn't mean a damn thing, she told herself sternly. *The hell it doesn't.* She told herself she had no business getting involved with anyone, and certainly not with someone she might fall for. *Do you think Blackhorn would hesitate to kill Treat, too?*

CHAPTER TWO

At her hotel, Treat began having second thoughts about dinner. She wasn't sure having dinner with Mickey was a good idea. But the thought of spending another evening alone in her hotel room held even less appeal.

Later, after showering, she put on gray slacks and a pale pink long-sleeve silk shirt. The decision of what to wear had taken a half hour even though she'd only brought two pairs of dressy slacks and two shirts because she'd only planned to be gone for two or three days and certainly hadn't thought she'd be having a date with a gorgeous woman. She resisted the urge to change her outfit and finished dressing. She thought she might be having first-date jitters, but she wasn't sure it was a first date. Actually, she wasn't sure it was even a date.

Treat made sure she had the piece of wood with the directions on it. She was directionally challenged and without directions would be lost when she left the parking lot. She grabbed a sweater from her suitcase and left the hotel.

Treat stopped at the Guilford Country Store, a small mom-and-pop grocery store at the edge where two roads crossed. For most people living in the area, the Country Store served as the heart of Guilford. The store carried only the essentials, bread, beer, chips, milk, sometimes locally grown vegetables, as well as the local gossip. Despite its lack of items for sale, the store was a hubbub of activity.

All conversation stopped when Treat stepped inside. Little had changed in the six years since she'd been in the store with Chloe. Men were standing around gossiping and enjoying a beer. She noted the owner had added a few chairs and a potbelly stove. Although the stove served as a table top now, in a month or two, she was sure it would be fired up and serve as the source of the store's warmth. She knew she was being assessed by the seven men smoking and drinking. She wondered how long it would take someone to ask who she was.

"Are you new to town? I haven't seen you around, have I?" the owner asked as Treat made her way toward the drink cooler along the back wall.

"No. I'm new."

"You building the house out in the meadow?" one of the beer drinkers asked.

Treat nodded.

"Gonna live there year-round or are you a summer resident?" another man asked.

Treat hesitated, her natural reluctance to talk about her personal life having kicked in at the first question. However, she knew these guys were going to be her neighbors, so she lowered her guard, but only a tiny bit.

"Year-round."

"Good," one man said, and the others nodded.

"The summer residents are a pain in the ass," another told her.

She must have passed some sort of test because the men introduced themselves.

When she told them what her name was, she expected

comments on her unusual first name. Instead, they all welcomed her to the neighborhood. Treat remembered the area was known for having been a hippie haven during the 1970s, and she expected these men had heard their share of strange names.

Treat paid for the large bottle of sparkling water she'd chosen from the drink cooler, and smiled at the owner, who blushed. As she walked out the door, she was followed by several men calling "See ya later, Treat."

Treat waved at them and was still smiling as she got into her car. She only got lost once on her way to Mickey's in spite of the detailed directions. She'd need another visit or five to be able to find her destination without the piece of wood now lying on the drink holders between the front seats.

Despite having to turn around and retrace her route, she still ended up in front of Mickey's house early. She sat in her car and had decided to leave when Mickey came out of the house and headed down the gentle incline toward her. "Damn it! Look at her. Who could resist her? Who'd want to?" she muttered to herself.

❖

Mickey was washing the utensils and cutting boards she'd used to prepare dinner when Treat parked at the gate leading to her house. When Treat didn't get out of the car, Mickey wondered what she should do. "Damn it, she's going to drive off if I don't go get her out of the car," she said under her breath. She dried off her soapy hands and rushed out to get Treat.

❖

Treat watched Mickey, who was wearing a pair of black Levi's and a red T-shirt, come out of her house. Treat was captivated watching Mickey stride toward her. She wondered what about Mickey spoke so deeply to her. Whatever it was, it was sexy as hell.

"I've been watching for you. I'm so glad you decided to come. When you didn't get out of your car, I was afraid you'd change your mind and drive off," Mickey said.

"The thought occurred to me."

"You're here now, though. C'mon, I'm ready to put the steaks on the grill."

Treat handed her the bottle of sparkling water she'd bought at the store.

"Thanks. You didn't need to bring anything," Mickey said as she touched Treat's arm.

When Mickey moved her hand, Treat could feel where Mickey's fingers had been. *This is not good, Treat. Eat dinner, go home, and forget this woman.*

As they climbed the five steps to Mickey's deck, a chocolate Labrador puppy came gamboling out of the house and skidded to a stop when she saw a stranger standing with Mickey. She tentatively wagged her tail at Treat. *Who could possibly resist that?* Treat climbed the steps and sat down on the top one. Instantly, the puppy was in her lap reaching up to kiss her face. Treat laughed out loud as the soft pink tongue glided over her cheek. She could smell the familiar smell of puppy breath.

"What's her name?" Treat asked.

"I don't know yet. I only picked her up yesterday from the breeder. I thought I'd wait a couple of days until a name that fits her comes to me. In the meantime, she'll respond to whatever you call her. I've been calling her Baby," Mickey said with a smile.

"Well, Baby, it's a very apt name. You're very, very sweet."

As they ate dinner, Treat thought, not for the first time, there was nothing quite like the taste of a grilled steak, especially when it was prepared by someone else. They ate at a table, with tablecloth and candles, on the deck. If she hadn't known better, she'd have said Mickey was wooing her. *Wooing? Did you just use the word "wooing"? Good Lord, Treat, get hold of yourself!*

"Why did you choose to build in Vermont?" Mickey asked.

"I've owned the property for years and decided it was time to either sell it or build on it. I couldn't bear to sell it."

"It's a beautiful piece of land. I love the house, too."

"Thanks. What brought you to Vermont?"

"I've been here for years. Where do you live now?"

Treat was aware they both moved the conversation away from themselves. She knew why she was doing it and wondered why Mickey was doing the same.

"Dinner was delicious. Thank you for inviting me to share," Treat said, pleased with the adroit segue to a safe topic of conversation.

"You're welcome. I enjoyed your company."

"Let me help with the dishes," Treat said.

"I'll take care of them. Why don't you get comfortable in one of the chaise lounges," Mickey said, nodding toward a grouping of chairs.

The chairs faced the woods. Baby crawled into her lap and snuggled down. Treat could hear Mickey moving around behind her as she transferred the dishes from the dinner table to the kitchen. Treat laid her head back and closed her eyes. She listened to the noises made by the creatures in the woods. Between a full stomach, the sounds emanating from the woods, the puppy between her legs with its head on her thigh, and a beautiful woman in the kitchen, she could feel herself relaxing and getting drowsy.

❖

Mickey smiled when the puppy, without so much as a by your leave, crawled up between Treat's legs and lay down. Mickey took the dishes inside before she got even more maudlin. This was new for Mickey. For three years, she'd held every woman she met at arm's length. Treat, though, was something else altogether. Something was alluring about the woman. She'd like to find out more about her. She knew she had no business getting involved with her, and she wouldn't, but it wouldn't hurt to learn more about this incredibly sexy woman.

❖

Treat heard Mickey come out of the house. She didn't open her eyes, but could sense Mickey standing beside her.

"It's so peaceful out here," Treat whispered.

"Yes, it is. This is one of the reasons why I moved up here."

"Where did you move from?"

"DC."

"What are the other reasons you moved here and away from the hustle and bustle of DC?"

Treat could sense Mickey's reluctance to talk about what else had motivated her to leave DC. She didn't want to push Mickey too far for fear the woman would clam up entirely.

"Want to talk about it?" Treat asked.

"Not really."

Mickey settled into a nearby chair. Baby left Treat for Mickey. They continued talking but neither would—or could—answer any personal questions.

An hour later, Treat stood up. "I need to be going. I'm returning to California tomorrow."

"Are you going to be gone long?" Mickey looked away from Treat and said, "The Vermont Marriage Initiative is having a fund-raising dance next Saturday here in Bratt, and I thought you might like to go with me. I mean, it'll be a good way of meeting people here in town. If you're going to be in town." She trailed off, sounding flustered.

Mickey smiled hopefully. Treat's heart did a somersault when dimples on either side of the smile came into view. She wasn't used to having such a visceral reaction to a woman's smile. *What the hell are you doing to me, Mickey Heiden?*

"I'll be sure to be back in time for the dance," Treat said.

"Great. It's semiformal, and don't forget to bring your best dancing shoes with you when you come back."

"I'll have to find them first."

"Please don't change your mind about going to the dance with me."

"I won't. I promise," Treat said, surprising herself.

A soft breeze came out of the nearby woods and blew a strand of Treat's hair onto her forehead, Mickey started to reach toward Treat but stopped when Treat shivered.

"Are you cold?"

"A little. I've got a sweater in the car. But I need to be going."

"I understand," Mickey said.

Mickey set the sleepy puppy down and walked Treat to her car. After Treat opened her door, she paused long enough to brush her lips against Mickey's cheek. "Thanks for dinner, Mickey."

Mickey smiled. "You're welcome."

"See you soon."

"Call me when you get back to town, you've got my number on the map," Mickey said, pointing with her chin to the piece of wood sitting on the passenger seat.

"I will, and thanks for a beautiful evening," Treat said, as she got into her car.

❖

Mickey wasn't sure whether she was relieved Treat was leaving or disappointed. Probably both, she decided. She turned back toward the house. As she washed the dishes, she thought about Treat. She was happy Treat had agreed to go to the dance with her on Saturday. *Oh, my God. What will I wear? Levi's won't do. Maybe...* Before she could get too far down the road, she stopped herself. She'd figure out what to wear on Saturday morning like she'd always done.

Chapter Three

Treat returned to Brattleboro Friday afternoon and checked back into the Latchis Hotel. Once in her room, she picked up her phone to call Mickey but returned it to the charger. *What am I going to say to her? She asked you to call her,* she reminded herself. Again, she picked up the phone, and again put it back down. Before she could pick up her cell phone a third time, the room telephone rang, startling her and making her heart race. She picked up the phone but didn't say anything. She expected it to be the hotel desk calling.

"Treat?" Mickey asked.

"Mickey?"

"Yep. How are you? How was California? How long have you been back?" Mickey asked in a rush.

"I'm fine. California was warm and smoggy. I only got in about an hour ago."

"Can you have dinner with me tonight?"

"Yep," Treat said. *God, now I'm talking like her.*

"If you come out here, I'll cook for you again. Baby's been asking for you."

"Has she, now? Has she grown?"

"Wait till you see her. You won't believe how much she's changed. Can you be here at six?"

"Yep."

"You're making fun of me, right?"

"A little. I need to shower and change clothes. I'm hanging up now so I can be there by six."

"See you soon. Baby says to hurry."

Treat laughed and hung up.

Later, Treat looked around Mickey's home as she entered through French doors. She was taken by the beauty of the house. There was only a single room with a tall cathedral ceiling with exposed beams. The living room was to her left. It had a large stone fireplace with huge windows on either side of it. Next to the living room, and separated from it by a beautiful Japanese folding screen, was the bedroom. She moved on to the huge kitchen. Denis, her California housekeeper/best friend, would love this kitchen. In the middle, there was a wooden island large enough to accommodate a sink even Treat knew was for washing vegetables. Separating the kitchen from the rest of the house were two waist-high bars at ninety degrees of each other with room for four stools. All in all, the effect was stunning, rustic but elegant. *Like the owner.*

There were several wood carvings displayed on a shelving unit on the wall opposite the kitchen. Treat walked over to get a closer look. Three of them were of women's faces.

"I carved them from the knots lumber companies toss aside," Mickey said from behind her, "before grinding them up for sawdust."

"They're beautiful."

"Thanks. Come talk to me while I finish fixing dinner."

Treat turned toward Mickey in time to catch Mickey running her eyes down her body and back up again to meet her eyes. A ribbon of pleasure hit Treat when a flash of desire appeared in Mickey's eyes.

"Nice shoes," she said in an attempt to cover her embarrassment at being caught lusting after her dinner guest.

Treat laughed out loud. She had worn a pair of bubblegum pink Reebok high-tops.

Mickey beat a hasty retreat to the kitchen, giving Treat a chance to admire her body.

After dinner, they again sat out on the deck. This time, though, they both wore sweaters against the chill. Treat could see stars in the dark sky above them. She'd never lived any place where she could see stars at night.

Treat was startled when Mickey gently covered her hand. "Hey, where'd you go?"

"I was admiring your sky. I was trying to remember the last time I saw stars. I don't have an answer."

"You can come over any time and admire my sky, but I think you'll have a similar view from your own backyard. When are you moving in?"

"Soon. I have to buy some furniture because I don't have a stick of it."

"Aren't you having your stuff moved out from California?"

"No. I'm leaving everything there."

"Trying to hedge your bets? In case rural life isn't for you? Or is this place just a vacation home?"

"I hadn't thought of it in quite those terms, but you may be right. I think I'm trying to start over here. New sky, new state, new house, new furniture, new life."

"What are you running away from in California that would have you hiding out in rural Vermont?" Mickey asked, hoping it was not another woman.

"For starters, when I was there this time, I finalized the sale of my business, and if I stayed in California, the new owners would have the option of calling on me for advice. I'm through with the business, and the new owners, who are former employees, know it as well as I do, so they don't really need me. I'd only be a crutch for them."

"What kind of business was it?" Mickey asked.

"It's a security company. Taylor and Dandridge."

"I know you're the Dandridge. Who is the Taylor?"

"She was my lover," Treat said quietly.

Treat watched as Mickey's face went from being open to being closed off in a matter of seconds, like a door slamming shut.

"When will she be joining you?"

"She won't."

"I'm sorry," Mickey said. "Did she not want to move here?"

"She died three years ago."

Mickey reached over and put her hand on Treat's arm. "I'm really sorry for your loss, Treat."

Treat looked at Mickey and saw real caring in her eyes and believed she was genuinely sorry. Treat wondered if she knew what it felt like to lose someone she loved.

Treat tried to stifle the yawn that came upon her with no warning. She wasn't fast enough, though, to keep Mickey from seeing it. She hoped Mickey couldn't see her blushing. *My God, you haven't blushed since you were fourteen.*

"Am I boring you?" Mickey asked with a smile.

"Not in the least. I'm just tired. I've been up since six yesterday morning. I don't do well without my eight hours."

"No wonder you're yawning."

Treat heard some relief in Mickey's voice, but couldn't understand the why of it.

"In any event, it is getting late, and I should be going," Treat told Mickey as she stood up. "Thanks again for dinner. When I get my house furnished, you'll have to let me cook dinner for you."

"That's a deal. If you need help with the furnishings, let

me know. I know all the good furniture places around here and could lend you a hand."

"I thought I'd go to Boston for a few days and shop till I drop."

"That will work, too."

Mickey walked Treat to her car and opened the door for her. She brushed her lips lightly over Treat's cheek before stepping away. Treat knew if she hadn't been so tired, she would have demanded more from Mickey than a brief kiss on the cheek. *Maybe it's because I'm so tired that I want more.*

Before closing Treat's door, Mickey asked, "Will you have dinner with me tomorrow night before the dance?"

"Of course," Treat said.

"I'll pick you up at seven, then."

"I look forward to it."

Treat only barely managed to stay awake on the short trip back to the hotel. She stopped by the desk to check for messages and was relieved there were none.

In her room, she thought briefly about calling Denis to see how things were going in the aftermath of her departure but decided he didn't need her checking up on him. Instead, she pulled the covers down on the bed and sat down to take her shoes off.

The next thing Treat knew, it was morning and the sun was shining brightly through the windows. She didn't remember getting out of her clothes, but she had. Surprisingly, they were hung neatly over the back of the chair at the desk. *Old habits die hard*, she thought, thankful for old habits. She glanced at the clock by her bed and was startled to see it was already ten o'clock. She couldn't remember the last time she had slept past seven o'clock. *Damn, this place does strange things to you. Don't forget the issue of the time zones. It's really seven a.m. in California.* She felt better about sleeping so late with that justification.

Treat walked around town after getting a bagel and cream cheese at the local bagel shop near the hotel. She stepped into one store, Vermont Artisans Design, in the center of town, and saw a rocking chair that, once she sat in it, she had to have. It was so comfortable she was loath to get out of it. She paid an exorbitant price for comfort and arranged to have two of the chairs delivered to her house.

Treat returned to the hotel at midafternoon to make calls to California before her date with Mickey. Afterward, she decided to treat herself to the luxury of a long soak in the tub using lavender bath salts she'd purchased during her saunter around downtown.

CHAPTER FOUR

That evening, Treat was waiting in the lobby of the hotel when Mickey strode in. Mickey didn't see her immediately, so Treat was able to study her for a brief few moments. Mickey wore a navy blue suit with a collarless white shirt that was unbuttoned to show a hint of the firm breasts beneath the cotton. Treat had only seen Mickey in jeans and T-shirts until now. Dressed in a power suit, Mickey was stunningly handsome.

Mickey finally found Treat and swiftly crossed the room to give her a kiss on the cheek. She whispered, "You're beautiful."

Treat's cheeks colored slightly at the compliment.

"I hope you like Chinese food. The best restaurant in town is the Chinese place, Panda North."

"I do love Chinese," Treat said.

Once they were on the road, Mickey asked, "Have you come to terms with the limitations on eating out here?"

Treat laughed, "No, not yet. There are many things I haven't yet come to terms with, though. Not the least is the lack of real restaurants. I notice the area doesn't lack for fast food options, though."

"It took me a couple of months to figure it out. After a

while, though, you get used to it, and it no longer seems as important as it was when you first moved here. The good news is I had to teach myself to cook. I now have quite the cookbook collection."

"That's the good news? I don't see myself learning to cook."

"You won't have any choice. When winter comes, and you can't leave your driveway, even the fast food places won't be an option for you."

"Oh. Yeah. I forgot about winter."

"I know my grandmother is rolling over in her grave."

"Why?"

"She tried to get me to learn how to cook, but I was too busy being a jock."

Panda North was located on the northern outskirts of Brattleboro. Treat studied the menu, impressed with the variety of dishes available. After mentally choosing four or five items she wanted to order, and being unable to narrow it down, she said, "I can't make up my mind."

"I was the same way when I first came here. Everything on the menu is delicious. Why don't we share something? My favorite is the tangerine shrimp with shrimp fried rice for the entrée and the California rolls as an appetizer."

"Thank God. I could have sat here most of the evening trying to decide what to order," Treat said with a laugh.

Dinner was unhurried, and they lingered at their table, drinking endless cups of jasmine tea and talking about safe, non-personal topics.

Afterward, the parking fairy was with them, and they found a space in the Harmony Lot in the center of town. They walked across the street to the fund-raiser being held in the River View Gallery—by day an art gallery and, on this night, an open-air bistro. By the time Mickey and Treat arrived, the place was crowded. As they entered, heads turned to watch them.

❖

Mickey saw the heads turning their way. She wondered what Treat was thinking. Earlier in the evening, she remembered telling her she was beautiful, and the resultant blush had amused Mickey no end. *Does no one tell this woman she's beautiful? How could they not? I am obviously not the only one who thinks she's gorgeous if the number of people staring at her is any indication.*

❖

Mickey led them to the line in front of the table where tickets were being taken and propaganda handed out. Mickey tensed as she stared intently out the front windows. A man in the shadows across the street was leaning against the wall near the store where Treat had bought her rockers that morning. As if sensing Mickey staring at him, he walked out of the shadows, arrogantly tipped his hat and walked up the street and out of sight.

"Who was that?" Treat asked.

"No one. I thought I knew him, but I don't."

Treat didn't believe Mickey didn't know the man because she'd felt Mickey tense when she realized she was being watched. And the man had tipped his hat to her. Treat was concerned because her internal alarms were ringing, which usually meant danger was at hand.

The line moved, and they were at the table. Mickey gave the woman in front of her the tickets, and they were allowed into the fund-raiser.

Several people said hello to Mickey as they made their way toward the bar. Other women were staring at Mickey, and Treat wondered how many of them she had slept with.

Before they could get to the bar, a woman stood up and waved at Mickey. Mickey detoured to the table near the dance floor. After introductions were made, Mickey pulled a chair out for Treat and whispered in her ear she would get them drinks, adding "the usual?" Treat nodded yes even as she wondered about her visceral reaction to feeling Mickey's breath on her ear.

When Mickey returned with their drinks, she put them on the table and held her hand out to Treat. "Dance?"

Wordlessly, Treat stood and followed Mickey to the dance floor. Mickey turned and held her arms open. As Treat moved into the circle of Mickey's arms, it was as natural as breathing.

The music was slow and sensual, with an alto sax crooning into the still night air. Mickey pulled Treat closer and rested her cheek lightly next to Treat's, but what made Treat's stomach gyrate was Mickey's thighs pressed against hers.

"You smell lovely," Mickey whispered in her ear.

Treat wasn't sure enough of her voice to answer, and the only thing she knew for sure was she hoped the music would never stop. But end it did. As Treat took a step away from Mickey, she was surprised to note the wisp of desire in Mickey's eyes. As a fast song began to play, Mickey took Treat's hand and led her back to their table. When they reached the table, Treat was faced with ten pairs of eyes and a barrage of questions.

The ten women at the table wanted to know all about Treat, but she, with years of practice, was able to give them enough information about herself to satisfy their curiosity without divulging anything of importance. Mickey sat back watching the interaction of Treat and the other women. When another slow song started, Mickey asked Treat to dance before any of the other women could—much to the disappointment of half the table.

Again, she pulled Treat close once they were on the dance floor. Treat was almost glad to know her reaction to being in Mickey's arms the first time was not an anomaly because she was certainly feeling it again.

"You don't give out much information about yourself, do you?" Mickey asked.

"I beg your pardon," Treat said with a smile, "I answered every one of their questions."

"With the barest amount of information possible. When they compare notes later, they'll realize all they really know about you is you're from California, you bought property in Guilford, and built a house. Not much info there, Treat."

"You sound disappointed."

"I am. All I know about you is you're from California, you bought property in Guilford, and built a house," Mickey said with a laugh.

"You've got all the important stuff, then," Treat told her with a smile.

"Not really."

"What is it you think you're missing?"

"For starters, are you with someone?"

"I told you last night my lover died."

"Didn't you also say she died three years ago?"

"I did."

"And there hasn't been anyone since then?"

"I've dated, but nothing serious since Chloe."

"You must have loved her a great deal."

"More than life itself."

Treat knew Mickey was surprised at the answer, but it was the truth. She wouldn't lie to Mickey about Chloe and her feelings for her.

Treat let Mickey pull her closer and hold her tightly as if to take away some of the pain Treat was unable to hide.

Mickey said, "Treat, do you want to go somewhere quiet and talk?"

Treat was torn between wanting to be with Mickey and not wanting to have to talk about Chloe. "I think so."

"You don't sound like you want to leave. We can stay if you want."

"No, Mickey, I want to leave. But I can't talk about Chloe."

Mickey hesitated.

"Please, Mickey, let's get out of here," Treat whispered.

Mickey took her hand and led her through the throng of partygoers to the door.

"Want me to drive? Or do you want to go back to your hotel?"

"You drive."

They crossed the street and found Mickey's SUV in the lot. Once inside, Mickey asked, "Where do you want to go?"

"Can we go out to my place?"

"Of course," Mickey answered as she started the car.

They drove in companionable silence during the fifteen minutes it took them to get to Treat's new home. Treat glanced in the side mirror and saw a white car behind them. She wondered about it briefly, then thought nothing more of it.

"I thought you weren't going to take possession until next Tuesday."

"My local attorney called and said the certificate of occupancy had been issued earlier than expected and I could move the signing up to early this afternoon if I wanted. So I did. The place is mine now."

"Let's go see it, then."

Treat noted Mickey parked her car in the shadows cast by the big oak near her front door, effectively hiding it from anyone driving by her house. Treat made a mental note to ask her why she did that.

Treat let them in with her newly minted key. There was enough light from the full moon pouring through the skylight for them to see where they were going. Treat found a light switch and flipped it on. A large pile of plastic bags was in the corner of the foyer.

"Out shopping, were you?"

"I'm really sick of the hotel and bought just enough so I'd be able to stay here until I can get to Boston to do the rest of my shopping."

"When are you going shopping?"

"I don't know. I can't seem to get myself motivated to do it."

"Why don't we do it together? I need some stuff myself."

"You don't have to do that."

"I know, but I want to," Mickey said putting her hand on Treat's arm. "What did you buy today?"

"Not much. You know, one of those inflatable beds, towels, toilet paper, all the necessities."

Treat went into the living room and stood looking out the French door across the meadow just beyond. "I love this view for some reason."

Mickey moved behind her and nuzzled Treat's neck, putting her arms around Treat's waist. Treat stiffened.

Mickey took a step away. "Sorry."

"Maybe this wasn't such a good idea, Mickey."

"What isn't such a good idea?"

"The dance. Our being here."

"Why not?"

"Because this is very scary for me."

"Why?"

"Why? Because you scare me."

"What? I scare you? How is that?"

"It just is."

"Now that's an infantile evasion if ever I've heard one," Mickey said with a smile.

"You're right, it is. But it's the best I can do when you're standing so close. My mind begins to turn to mush and my ability to provide brilliant repartee disappears."

Mickey chuckled. "I can understand that. I've been unable to concentrate on much of anything since I first saw you. All I can think about is when I'm going to see you again."

"Really?"

"Why does it surprise you? I've done everything but fall down on my knees begging you to spend time with me."

Treat smiled broadly. "Would you fall down on your knees and beg?"

"In a New York nanosecond if I thought it would do any good."

Treat wasn't sure whether it was true. She wasn't even sure yet whether she could trust Mickey. What she was sure of, though, was the vision of Mickey on her knees in front of her made her heart beat like a runaway train.

CHAPTER FIVE

Tell you what, Treat. Why don't we go upstairs, set up the inflatable bed, dim the lights, and have dessert? We can talk all night because I want to know more about the mysterious Treat Dandridge and why she would move three thousand miles from an urban setting to rural Vermont at the drop of a hat. By the way, I hope I can borrow a pair of sweats if you've got an extra set."

"You're in luck. I do have an extra pair. And because I like you, I'll even throw in a T-shirt."

"Now you're talking. I've got drinks in a cooler in my truck and snacks I picked up for a book club meeting tomorrow afternoon. I'll be right back."

When Mickey reentered the house, Treat could hear her as she climbed the stairs juggling the drinks and snacks. When Mickey got to the top of the stairs, she called, "Treat?"

Treat emerged from the room on the right side of the hallway. She wore a pair of black sweatpants and blue T-shirt with Donald Duck on the front. From the look on Mickey's face, she knew Mickey surmised she looked out of place in her sweats and T-shirt.

"You've got to love Walmart for the fashions," Mickey told her as she entered the bedroom.

Treat looked down at Donald and grinned. "Hey, I'm a big fan of this guy. Don't knock the Duck. Your clothes, by the way, are on the inflatable bed box."

Mickey put down the things she was carrying, picked up the sweatpants and T-shirt, and stepped into the bathroom to change.

When Mickey came out with her neatly folded suit and shirt, she was wearing a pair of black sweats that were too short and a red T-shirt with Minnie Mouse on it that was too small.

"Before you say a word, you need to know Minnie and I have been friends since she and I were much younger. I feel better already. How about you?"

Treat was already taking the bed out of the box, which was no easy task. Once she freed the bed, she gave a grunt of victory.

"Need help? I could at least read the instructions," Mickey said.

"No. I've almost got it," Treat told her, knowing it was far from the truth.

Mickey sat cross-legged on the floor, reading the instructions to herself and watching Treat struggle with the bed. Finally, Treat threw in the towel.

"I'm defeated. Read me the damn instructions."

Mickey laughed and together they got the bed inflated. It took only a minute to put sheets on it and pillowcases on the pillows. They each took a can of soda from Mickey's cooler. Mickey fixed a plate of cheese and crackers, and they settled on the bed catty-corner from one another, their backs resting against a wall and their feet almost touching.

"Okay," Mickey told Treat. "Ask me anything."

Treat decided to start with the easy stuff.

"What is Mickey short for?"

"Damn, and I thought this might be hard. Mickey is short for Michael."

"Really? Where did your name come from?"

"My mother was a huge fan of the actress Michael Learned, and it was my paternal grandfather's name. She named me that to get my father's mother off her case about using their last name for my middle one. When I was really small, she started calling me Mickey, and it stuck. My turn."

Treat tried not to erect mental walls against the questions that were coming, but it was hard. She liked the woman sitting across from her, but she didn't trust her enough yet to give too much of herself.

"How did you come by your name?"

The question surprised Treat. She would have bet money Mickey's questions would be about Chloe even after telling her she wouldn't talk about Chloe.

"Treat is the middle name of nearly every firstborn girl on my mother's side going back at least a couple of generations. My father's parents objected to the name. I'm only glad my mom wasn't pissed enough at her in-laws to name me something like Susie Sunshine!" Treat said, laughing.

"Why, after three years, has someone not swept you off your feet? Why are you still alone? Surely the women in California have been falling all over you."

"Wait a second. It's my turn to ask the question."

"Answer my questions, please."

"I'm not exactly alone. I have a live-in housekeeper who, over the years, has become my best friend. To be truthful, I didn't want for company, but I wasn't interested. I needed to learn to live without Chloe before I even considered dating again. I've only been in one relationship in my entire life."

"Would you consider having another relationship like that?"

Treat knew another relationship like the one she had with Chloe wasn't possible. That one had been the one for her.

"I know one thing for certain right now, and that is I don't want a casual affair. I can have those, but I wouldn't find it satisfying."

"Would you consider settling down with one woman ever again?"

"I think so. I'd like to settle down with someone someday."

❖

Mickey wondered if Treat was talking about them. *You need to stay uninvolved and keep your distance from her. But... There are no buts here, Mickey. If you can't be honest with her, then you have no business getting involved with her. And you can't be honest with her. Honesty may get her killed. Is that what you want? More blood on your hands? Grace wasn't enough?*

❖

"Treat, I don't know whether I can give you what I think you're asking for. I don't know that I can have a long-term relationship with anyone. At least not right now."

Treat lowered her eyes so Mickey wouldn't see the disappointment she was feeling. When Mickey reached over and took Treat's hand in hers, she knew she hadn't been fast enough.

"Treat, look at me."

Treat hesitated long enough to get her business game face on. She wanted to hide the vulnerability she'd felt a moment earlier from talking about what she longed for and didn't think she'd ever have, a relationship with someone that would be similar to what she'd had with Chloe. Treat made sure there was only ice in her voice and eyes, and she did the only thing she knew how to do, take the offensive. "I wasn't talking about you, Mickey. I hardly know you. I was talking about women in California and in generalities." The two women sat looking at one another. Treat's mind raced to figure out what really had just happened. *Why are you so angry with her? Or are you angry with yourself for answering honestly? Did I jump to conclusions when none were warranted?* The one thing she was sure of was her reaction to Mickey's question had destroyed the easy camaraderie, the playfulness, and the intimacy.

"I'm sorry if I misread what you said, Treat. Maybe I should leave and go home." Mickey didn't look like she wanted to leave.

Treat felt a little less icy as she continued to look at Mickey. "I don't want you to leave," Treat whispered. She was uncertain what to do next. She wanted to regain the easiness between them but had no idea how to do it. Mickey was being no help at all.

Finally, Mickey got up from the bed and said, "Come on. We need to make a list of the things you need to buy. Do you have paper? If not, I've got a spare piece of wood in the truck."

While surprised by Mickey's list-making quest, Treat was relieved. She no longer wanted to bare her heart to Mickey Heiden. The potential for hurt was far too great. She knew she didn't have any paper in the house, so they'd have to settle for the Notes app on her iPhone.

It was nearly three o'clock Sunday morning by the time the two women had gone from room to room making a list of the items needed to furnish the large house. It had been fun. They bantered back and forth, and each studiously avoided talking about feelings.

"Who knew list making could be so exhausting?" Treat asked.

"I agree. I hope I can stay awake on the trip home."

"Why not stay here, then?"

"Treat, where would I sleep? It seems you have only one bed, and I am too old, too tired, and too hurt to sleep on the floor."

"We can share the bed. I don't know about you, but I'm so tired I couldn't do anything to anybody, even if I wanted to."

"I don't know, Treat."

"Suit yourself, Mickey, but I'm going to bed." Treat started up the stairs but paused and held out her hand. "Come on. I won't bite."

"Well, in that case, how can I refuse such an offer?"

Treat knew sleeping in the same bed with Mickey was a huge mistake, but she was powerless to deny wanting to be with Mickey for a while longer.

Treat awoke hearing the morning birds outside the open windows of her bedroom and watched the sun dance along the walls. The next thing she was aware of was Mickey's hand resting between her thighs, cupping her. There wasn't anything sexual about it, but nevertheless it was the most intimate feeling she'd had for a very long time. She knew she should move away, but she stayed, reveling in the moment. Slowly, she turned her head to look at Mickey, and her heart literally skipped a beat. Mickey was still asleep, and her golden brown eyelashes, thick and long, lay on her cheek. Her luscious lips were turned up in a slight smile. Treat wanted to run her finger over those lips and down the center of Mickey's T-shirt and beneath her sweats. Before she could change positions, the front doorbell rang.

Mickey jerked awake, and when she realized where her hand was, she yanked it away. She managed to look both surprised and guilty at the same time.

"Who the hell is ringing your doorbell?"

"Shit, I don't know. Very few people know I'm here. In any case, who would come calling at this hour on a Sunday morning?"

The doorbell rang again. Someone was apparently intent on speaking with her, so Treat got out of bed. Treat saw Mickey watching her. She continued to walk toward the bedroom door as she finger-combed her hair and pulled down her T-shirt. Treat had seen the desire and want in Mickey's eyes, but it didn't slow her pace toward the door. When she was in the hallway, she had to put her hand on the wall to keep herself upright. Her knees had been turned to jelly by the look in Mickey's eyes. Even so, she felt like she'd dodged a bullet. She had so wanted to make love with Mickey, and would have, but she was literally saved by the bell.

Treat moved slowly down the stairs to the front door, still in a trance. She pulled it open and was stunned to see Denis.

After giving him a long hug, she asked, "What are you doing here?"

"I missed you. I've come to see where you live. Are you going to invite me in?"

"Sorry. Yes, come in."

She stepped aside and allowed Denis to enter the foyer of her new home.

"Nice," Denis told her, looking around. "I want to see the rest."

Denis's eyebrows shot up to his hairline as he looked

over Treat's shoulder. Treat turned around and found Mickey, looking wonderfully rumpled and very sexy, standing on the bottom stair. Mickey had changed from the sweats of the evening before into the suit she had worn to the dance. She was carrying her shoes in her hand. Treat made the introductions.

"I've got to run, Treat," Mickey said and touched Treat on her shoulder as she headed for the front door.

"I'll be back in a minute," Treat told Denis as she turned to follow Mickey outside.

"Mickey?"

"What?"

"You don't need to go. We can go out for breakfast."

"No. Your friend came to see you. You need to be with him. Call me later. Otherwise, I'll see you bright and early Tuesday morning. You'll figure out how to get us to the stores in Boston, right?"

"I'll call you this evening. And yes, I'll figure out how to get us to Boston."

Treat leaned toward Mickey and brushed her lips across Mickey's. When she turned toward the house, Denis was watching them.

"Treat?"

Treat turned back to Mickey expectantly.

"You do know these kisses as we leave each other are never going to be enough for me, don't you?"

"They're already too little for me, Mickey," Treat whispered.

Treat turned and walked to the front door. Mickey stood watching Treat walk away from her.

As Treat entered the house, Denis said nothing about what he had seen. Instead, he said, "So show me the house."

They ended their tour in the living room. Treat motioned for Denis to follow her as she headed out the living room doors.

Denis said, "This is very impressive, Treat. It's very different from the California beach house but already feels like home. What say we go get you a decent refrigerator and stove? And some furniture?"

"Are you saying you're staying?" Treat asked incredulously.

"Only for a little while. I'll leave once you hire a replacement for me."

"Won't you stay on, Denis? I mean, we've been together for six years."

"No. I really can't stay in a town this small. I'm already feeling claustrophobic. I need restaurants and the theater. More than that, I need to know there's lots of hot guys waiting for me. I already know that's not true here."

"Oh, Denis. Are you sure?" Treat was devastated. She had thought if he came and saw Vermont and the new house, he'd stay. Apparently, it was not going to be the case. Ever the optimist, though, she vowed not to give him up without a fight.

"I am, girlfriend. I'm sorry, but I'm positive I'd be more than miserable here."

Treat didn't remind Denis there were no eligible men left in Orange County for him. He'd probably come to that conclusion on his own, which was why he was here in the first place. She wasn't yet willing to bury the hope Denis would move to Vermont with her.

Later, as Denis was busy getting his bags into his first-floor room, Treat stood in front of the French doors in the living room looking out over the large expanse of lawn at the rear of her house. She wondered what had happened to her life. Only a few short weeks earlier it had been ordered, even-keeled, and… *And what? And lonely.*

Treat's mind turned to Mickey, the beautiful, sexy Mickey. Something was troubling about Mickey, and that something was her unwillingness to talk about her past. Right now, her instincts were telling her Mickey was hiding something important, which usually meant, in Treat's line of work, something unpleasant. She mentally shrugged, knowing she couldn't know what Mickey was hiding until Mickey told her. She decided to wait and see if Mickey could learn to trust her. But she wasn't willing to wait forever.

Chapter Six

After she and Denis returned from their shopping trip to Brattleboro, they sat their bags down in the foyer. While Denis was putting his things away, Treat called Mickey. As she waited for Mickey to pick up, she moved into the living room and stood at the French doors. She wondered if she'd ever tire of the view—it wasn't that there was anything to see really, but it was a peaceful scene, and she could feel the stress melt away. She let Mickey's phone ring the obligatory five times, wondering why it wasn't going to voice mail. She was about to cut the connection when a woman's sleepy voice answered.

"Hello?"

"Mickey?"

"No."

"Is Mickey there?"

"No, she went out to get us ice cream, I think. She should be back any minute. Do you want to leave a message?"

"No thanks."

Treat was stunned. Mickey had another woman at her house. *Don't be stupid, of course she has another woman. She probably has dozens of women she can call who would go running to her. Do you really expect her to put her life on hold while you decide whether it's safe to be with her?*

Treat sometimes hated the rational voice inside her head, but too often the voice was right. *What were you expecting? That Mickey had a sudden insight you're the one she wants and needs? If this doesn't disabuse you of that notion, nothing will,* said the know-it-all voice. Treat had thought there might be a real connection between her and Mickey. She'd apparently thought wrong.

In the middle of the internal question-and-answer session, Denis walked into the living room. "So what do you country folk do for entertainment?"

"I don't know, Den. I haven't completed my transformation from city girl to country girl yet."

Denis walked over to stand next to Treat and try to see what was so interesting outside. There was nothing but a large expanse of green meadow leading to a forest. As far as he could see, there was nothing of note out there except grass and trees.

"What's going on, Treat?"

"Nothing."

"Come on, Treat. This is Denis you're talking to. We talk about everything. Remember? You've only been gone three days. You can't have forgotten how to share."

Treat smiled. It was true she did tell him everything. She presumed he did the same with her.

"I just called Mickey's house. A woman answered."

"Oh."

"Indeed."

"You understand you're jumping to conclusions at the speed of light about who the woman is, don't you?"

"Maybe. Maybe not."

"Is this thing serious with Mickey?"

"No."

"But?"

"But I think it could be."

"What's holding you back?"

"She doesn't trust me enough to talk about her past."

"You remember we can find out what's there, right?"

"I know, but I want her to tell me."

"And since she can't or won't tell you, you're going to keep her out of your life?"

"Wouldn't you?"

"You know, girlfriend, sometimes it's best if you don't talk about all the emotional stuff on the first dozen dates."

Treat didn't respond, but she did wonder if Denis was right.

The two stood silent for a moment staring out across the expanse of meadow. Treat heaved a deep sigh.

"Come on, Denis, I've got something to show you."

She opened the French doors and stepped outside. Denis followed her across the patio and onto a path hidden from anyone looking out from inside the house. The path meandered off to the right of the house and across the meadow. When they reached the edge of the meadow, the path continued into the woods.

Denis stopped dead in his tracks at the edge of the woods. "Are you sure it's safe to go in there?"

"Why wouldn't it be?"

"Well, there are probably bears and large snakes. And who knows how many other wild, vicious things in the forest."

"Denis, this is not a forest. Forests can stretch for miles. This is a copse, or for you novices, 'a woods.'"

"How do you know what it is?"

"My real estate agent told me."

"Of course," Denis said, laughing. "Where are we going?"

"Come with me, wussy boy. We're nearly there."

After a couple of minutes in the woods, with a very nervous Denis looking about searching for bears and other man-eating creatures, they stepped out of the woods and into a small clearing. There, in front of them, was another house. It was a two-story red brick home with green shutters hanging next to all the windows.

"What's this charming house doing stuck in the middle of the forest?"

"Woods. Let's check it out."

Treat went to the front door and inserted the key she took from her pocket. It was a simple five-room home, and it had the feeling of being easy to live in.

"This is delightful, Treat. What will you use it for?"

"I built it for you, Denis. I was hoping you'd move here with me. There's a road nearby we could extend to your front door, or you can use the road near my house. This way you'd have lots of privacy, some place of your own to do with as you wished, and wouldn't feel like you were sneaking your men into my home."

"I'm stunned and speechless, Treat. But as I said, I can't move here. Too rural for me, girlfriend. I'm so sorry."

"Nothing to be sorry about."

"I'm sure your next housekeeper will love this place."

"Not like you would, Denis."

"Perhaps your next housekeeper will be the rugged rural kind."

"Or perhaps she'll be the beautiful French maid kind."

"Or maybe he'll be the rugged French maid kind."

Treat and Denis laughed at the picture a lumberjack dressed in a French maid's costume conjured up.

As they returned to Treat's home, they tried to decide what to do next when Treat remembered the clerk at the hotel telling her about Keene, New Hampshire. They decided it was time to check out the largest nearby town and do some more shopping.

They spent the afternoon shopping and the evening talking about whatever popped into their minds. Much to their surprise, they were in bed at the indecently early hour of ten o'clock. Treat fell asleep thinking about Mickey. She was disappointed in Mickey, and she knew she had absolutely no right to be.

Chapter Seven

A t the ungodly hour of eight thirty the next morning, Treat's doorbell rang. Denis and Treat were in the kitchen enjoying their second cup of coffee.

"Delivery boys from someplace called Vermont Artisans Design are at the door with rocking chairs they say you bought," said Denis after answering the door. "Where do you want them?"

"In the living room. Denis, wait until you sit in one of them. They're divine."

Denis gave her a look that said there was no such thing as a divine rocking chair.

Once the delivery guys were gone, Treat and Denis decided to head to Boston to buy the furniture and appliances. Treat regretted not to be going with Mickey.

They spent the day shopping but decided at the end of the day they were too tired to drive back to Brattleboro and stayed overnight at the Copley Square Hotel.

Over breakfast the next morning, Denis asked, "What kind of car are you going to drive? You can't continue driving a rental."

"I want something big enough to haul stuff in and one that can manage the snow."

"Any particular make?" he asked.

"Not really."

Denis shook his head in disbelief. "You are such a girl."

"I suppose you know all about cars."

"More than you do, obviously."

"I suspect that between us, our knowledge of cars would fit into a Tonka truck."

Treat and Denis managed to navigate the business of buying a car with relative ease after Denis had spoken to the elderly hotel manager.

At the dealership, Treat left the negotiations to Denis after she'd chosen the car color she wanted. They drove off the lot with a new navy blue Escalade. Once they were out of Boston, the car all but drove itself. Treat had to admit it was a comfortable ride.

"What do you think?" Denis asked.

"You did good, boyfriend."

Denis smiled. "Thanks."

Three days later, on Friday, Treat watched Denis supervise the unloading of the last of the furniture and appliances from Boston. Treat was leaning against her new SUV, amused that Denis could bully men twice his size.

Treat heard the sound of a motor coming up her driveway. She wasn't expecting anyone. Her stomach gyrated because she wanted it to be Mickey. However, she didn't recognize the approaching SUV. After coming to a stop, a man got out and headed toward her.

"Are you, ah, Treat Dandridge?" he asked after consulting the clipboard in his hand.

"Yes, I am."

"Hi. I'm Frank Flushing. I'm with the Summerhill Kennels."

"How can I help you?"

"I have a delivery to make."

"I didn't order anything."

Frank laughed. "No, you didn't. This is a gift."

"A gift?"

"Wait till you see her. Then maybe you'll understand."

Frank went to the back of his SUV and opened the tailgate. He leaned into the back of the car, then reappeared carrying a squirming puppy—a chocolate Lab puppy.

"This is your gift, and here's the card to go with it," he said, handing her a small white envelope.

"I can't accept a puppy!"

"It seems you don't have much of a choice. She's paid for and registered in your name, so she's yours."

Frank put the squirming puppy in Treat's arms, handed her some papers, and returned to his car. Before Treat could get her head around the fact that someone had given her a puppy, Flushing was back in his car driving down the driveway.

The puppy settled down in Treat's arms. As she turned to go into the house, one of the gigantic moving guys approached Treat and gently petted the puppy.

"Bella, bella," he said softly.

Treat smiled at him, and he returned to the truck to grab another piece of furniture. She not only had a new puppy, but the puppy already had a name—Bella.

Denis, standing beside the front door supervising the men unload the truck, watched Treat heading toward him.

"What is that?" he asked as if she held an alien creature in her arms.

"It's a puppy, you idiot."

"I know it's a puppy, but what's it doing here?"

Treat had a good idea who the puppy was from, but she shrugged and said, "I don't know yet. I haven't read the card."

"You need to stay out of our way. We men have serious work to do and can't be watching out for the two of you."

Treat smiled at him and went through the house to the patio out back. She sat the puppy on the ground. The puppy bounced out to the grass where she chased imaginary creatures hiding there as well as a butterfly or two who were living dangerously by flying within the puppy's range.

Treat was ridiculously happy to have the puppy. When she looked at the small creature, her heart swelled. She'd never had a pet—even as adults, she and Chloe had thought they were too busy to give a pet, even a cat, the attention it needed. Now she had a pet, and Bella made her happy. She only wished she had thought to buy Bella for herself.

She sat on the ground and opened the card the breeder had given her. It said, *Lucy needs a playmate. Can we come over sometime?* It was signed *Mickey.* Treat had to blink back tears at the sweetness of the note and Mickey's generosity.

The puppy came gamboling up to Treat, and with a mighty leap jumped up, but missed Treat by several inches. Treat laughed at the puppy's antics. She lay basking in the grass enjoying the puppy, the warm sun, and the peace she felt. When the puppy curled up beside her, she could feel herself relax to the point of nearly falling asleep.

❖

When Mickey had arrived, Denis had told her where to find Treat. She had come around the corner of the house in time to see the puppy trying to jump in Treat's lap. She was pleased by Treat's joyous laughter and enormously pleased with herself for having thought of the gift. She watched as Treat lay back on the grass and closed her eyes. The puppy stirred, got up, and moved between Treat's outstretched legs to climb on Treat, walking delicately up her torso before lying down with her nose nuzzled beneath Treat's chin. The puppy promptly fell asleep. Mickey longed to be with Treat for the rest of her life but had a thousand reasons why it was a very bad idea.

❖

Treat, sensing she was no longer alone, gently moved the sleeping puppy onto the grass and sat up. She looked around and saw Mickey. She sprang to her feet. As Mickey moved toward Treat, Lucy came bounding around the corner and headed straight for Bella. The two puppies checked one another out. They had a mock battle full of puppy growls and barks that had the two women laughing in moments.

"Thank you for the gift, Mickey. She's wonderful."

"You're welcome. Do you have a name for her yet?"

"Bella."

"Bella? That's perfect."

The two women watched in silence as the puppies continued to romp with one another.

"I thought we were going shopping in Boston together Tuesday. When I came over, you weren't home. What happened?"

"I decided not to wait until Tuesday. Denis and I went down to Boston on Monday."

"A phone call would have been nice, Treat."

"I called you Sunday afternoon."

"You didn't leave a message."

"No."

"You're mad at me, aren't you?"

"Mad? No."

"Something's the matter. We had a date for Tuesday, and you didn't even bother to let me know you'd called it off. I'd say something was the matter."

"It's nothing, Mickey. Let it go."

"No, it is not 'nothing,' Treat," Mickey said and moved closer to Treat. "Please tell me what upset you."

When Mickey put her hand on Treat's arm, it sent a shock through the core of Treat's body. Involuntarily, she took a step away from Mickey.

Mickey looked at her quizzically. "Treat, what did I do? You won't even let me touch you."

"Mickey, it's not you."

"If it's not me, what the hell is it?"

Treat took a deep breath and decided to tell Mickey the truth.

"When I called Sunday afternoon, a woman answered your phone."

"Yeah, so?"

Treat knew she couldn't say anything else without looking childish, petty, and way out of line, so she said nothing. She stood in front of Mickey looking at her. Part of her mind was admiring Mickey's full lips and wondering how they would feel on her breast. *Stop right now*, she told herself, trying only somewhat successfully to think about anything other than Mickey's body. Mickey was way too close for her to think about anything else.

"Wait a second. You're upset because I had someone with me Sunday afternoon?"

"Yes," Treat said quietly.

"Listen, Treat, we're not in a relationship. Hell, we haven't even really kissed yet."

Treat was shocked at how much Mickey's simplistic take on the situation hurt even though what she said was true.

"Treat, I'm sorry. That sounded harsher than I intended. You took me by surprise. I'm not sure what to say right now. I'm confused, to say the least. Why would you think I wouldn't be with someone else? You know I want you, and I think you want me, but you didn't seem interested in sleeping with me. What do you expect me to do?"

"Mickey, you're right. I have no right to make any assumptions about you. I know I'm very attracted to you, and I'm scared to fall for someone again. I did that once, and when she died, I wanted to die, too. The other morning, when I woke up next to you, I longed to make love. I did not want to answer the door. Then I called you, and you were already with another woman. My feelings were hurt because I thought you felt something for me." Treat paused, unsure whether to go on or stop. She took a deep breath and said quietly, "You didn't call me."

"I don't know why I didn't call when you didn't. I guess I was waiting for you to make the move. I didn't know you called on Sunday. Then I was disappointed when you didn't call Monday. I thought you had changed your mind and didn't want to see me again. Now that I've said that, I wasn't sure why you wouldn't see me again—only I felt that way."

Treat was about to tell Mickey that, to the contrary, she wanted to see Mickey every day for a very long time. Before she could get it out, though, Denis came out on the patio.

"Are either of you interested in dinner?" He paused, looking from woman to woman. "Ah, did I interrupt something?"

"Yeah," Treat told him.

"No," Mickey said.

"I'll just go inside. You two come in when you're through out here." He moved back inside.

"Treat, I don't know what you're asking from me. Do you know?"

"I'm not sure I'm asking for anything from you."

"It feels like you are, though. You got hurt and pissed off when you called my place and a woman answered the phone.

That sounds like you're jealous and possessive. Which means you've already formed expectations of me. I don't even know what those expectations are and I'm not sure that you do either. I certainly don't know whether I'm willing to meet them. In any case, you don't have the right to expect anything of me at this point."

Treat was trying to keep her anger in check. She was angry because Mickey had called her on her shit. She had made assumptions about how Mickey was feeling without bothering to ask her. She'd assumed Mickey felt the same way she did about monogamy and a whole host of other things. That was unfair, to say the least. Treat knew herself very well, but she knew nearly nothing about Mickey.

"Mickey, I haven't met anyone since Chloe I've cared for, and I had a visceral reaction to you the first time I saw you. I don't think I have any expectations of you. Not now. Frankly, my reaction to my phone call on Sunday was because I misinterpreted some of what you said to me. That, however, is my problem, not yours."

Mickey stood watching Treat. "I appreciate you're being truthful with me, Treat. Where do you want to go from here?"

"If ever I was going to equivocate, now would be the time. However, that's not something I want to do with you. I'll tell you my bottom line. I want to be with you, to make love to you for hours and hours, and I don't want to get hurt."

"At last we're on the same page because I want to be with you, to make love to you, and I won't hurt you." Mickey paused, took a deep breath and said, "Although I don't need to give you an explanation, I want to. The woman who answered my phone on Sunday was a friend. She had come to the book club meeting at my house. She said she needed a place to stay for a couple of days, so I gave her my couch."

Treat's relief was overwhelming. She wanted the

explanation to be true. They moved into each other's arms as if pulled by a magnet. Treat was the first to pull back. She put her hand softly on Mickey's cheek. Mickey took Treat's hand, turned it over, and kissed the palm as gently as if a butterfly had landed there. They looked into each other's eyes, and each read an unspoken promise.

The puppies took that moment to run between the two women.

"I know you haven't had the opportunity to buy food for Bella, so I took the chance I'd still be around for her dinner and brought enough food for both of them with me."

"Will you have dinner with us?"

"I would like nothing better."

"Let's go see what Denis has planned. We went grocery shopping yesterday, and I swear the man bought one of everything in the store."

Denis grinned at them when they entered the kitchen.

"What's for dinner, Denis?" Treat asked him, guessing from his grin he might have been watching them through the kitchen window.

"How many will there be?"

"There will be three if you'll join us."

"Hey, you got a real refrigerator and a stove and stuff," Mickey said as she entered the kitchen.

"Yeah, Sloan and a couple of guys came by this morning and hooked everything up."

Chapter Eight

As the two women left the dinner table and headed toward the living room, the two puppies followed at their heels. In the foyer, Mickey stopped and turned to face Treat. Mickey reached out and caressed her cheek. "I have to leave."

Treat was surprised. She thought they were spending the evening together, perhaps even the night. "Why? Why does it feel like you're running?"

"I am not running away, Treat. When I came over today, I didn't intend to stay more than an hour while the girls played. I have to be in Montpelier first thing in the morning."

Treat didn't try to hide her disappointment. "Damn it, Mickey. You could have told me earlier instead of letting me fantasize about tonight."

"Fantasies are a good thing," Mickey said, and added, "I know I should have told you, but it would have put a damper on the evening."

Treat started to say something, but Mickey took the step necessary to close the space between them. Without another word, Mickey put a hand on each side of Treat's face and kissed her. At first, it was a soft, gentle kiss. The intensity of the kiss increased as their bodies touched from their knees to their lips. Their breathing increased as their passion grew.

Treat could feel every millimeter where their bodies met. There was electricity running from her lips straight down her chest to her clit.

Treat broke the kiss and took a step back.

"If you keep that up, Mickey, I won't be able to stand, and I sure as hell won't let you leave."

"Treat, you've got to know I don't want to go. Please tell me you know that. Please."

Treat saw the passion-darkened eyes and knew for certain Mickey was telling her the truth.

"Yes, I know. It doesn't make it any easier to let you go, though."

"When can I see you again? I'll be in Montpelier for the next few days. Tell me you don't have to go to California any time soon."

Treat laughed. "No, I don't have to go to California this week. I'll be here when you get back."

"Promise?"

"I have no plans on going anywhere any time soon."

Mickey gently pulled Treat into her arms, gave her another soul-searing kiss, then she and Lucy were gone.

Treat leaned her forehead against the closed front door. Denis found her there, and right behind her Bella sat looking as if she had lost her best friend.

"Well, you two are a pair. Where's Mickey?"

"She had to leave. She's got a new job in Montpelier. I think she was going up there this evening but stayed to have dinner with us."

"What a sweetheart. It's time we had a heart-to-heart talk, Treat. I want to know what's going on between you and that woman."

They returned to the kitchen, where Denis freshened his coffee and made a cup of tea for Treat. Treat could not count the number of times this scene had been played out over the last six years. She and Denis had seen each other through some awful times as well as some wonderful times—they had shared all his new loves, his breakups, the death of Chloe—all over cups of coffee and tea. They took their drinks out to the patio so Bella could do her business before bedtime.

"What do you know about Mickey? You've told me what you two did, but nothing about her."

Treat looked at Denis as she thought about what she knew about Mickey.

"I know very little about her. She's a carpenter with Sloan's outfit. She's intelligent, well-spoken, and I can't wait to get her in bed."

"That's not much. We'll have to remedy that."

When Bella was ready to go inside, they sat in Treat's new rockers and she let Denis catch her up on the news of Orange County. They finally headed to their separate bedrooms at midnight.

Treat hadn't yet deflated her air mattress, so Bella took it as her own. Treat didn't have the heart to take the bed away from the puppy. She crawled thankfully into bed and had no sooner closed her eyes than her cell phone rang.

"Did I wake you?"

Treat's stomach did a somersault when she recognized Mickey's voice.

"No, I've just climbed into bed. Can't sleep?"

"No. I can't get you out of my mind."

"That's good to hear," Treat said with a laugh.

"I've got to tell you, Treat Dandridge, there's not another woman alive who affects me the way you do."

"I'm so glad to hear that because I feel the same about you."

"What are you doing today?"

"Changing the subject, are you?"

"Yes, I am."

"All right, then. Denis and I are returning to Boston—we apparently forgot a few things on our last trip. Although I find that hard to believe."

"Oh, okay. As long as you're not walking around Bratt by yourself. I don't want any of the local dykes sweeping you off your feet while I'm gone. I want to be the one sweeping you into my bed."

"What are you saying?" Treat asked.

"The minute I hit town, I'm coming to your house, swooping you and Bella into my truck, and we're coming to my house."

"Well, aren't you the confident one to think I will allow myself to be swooped by the likes of you."

"Yeah, I am. You may have forgotten the kiss we shared a couple of hours ago, but I haven't. I want you to keep the promise you made with that kiss."

"What did I promise?"

"That you and I would be making love at the first opportunity."

Treat laughed. "That was the first opportunity, and as I recall, you practically ran out the door."

"I didn't exactly run."

"It felt like you were running to me."

"Well, maybe I hurried a bit, but I did not run."

"Nevertheless, you left. Here I am in my very new, very large bed all by myself."

"Want some company?"

"What about Montpelier?" Mickey had texted her earlier to explain the job in Montpelier was a commission by a gallery there.

"Screw Montpelier."

"Really? I don't believe you."

"No, I can't really screw Montpelier."

"Well, then. You better get some sleep so you're full of wonderfully creative ideas for them."

"I know, but I don't want to say good-bye."

"Neither do I, but you should get some rest. By the way, what about Lucy? Where is she staying?"

"She's staying at a kennel in town."

"Why can't she stay here with Bella?"

"Would you mind? I could drop her off tomorrow morning on my way out of town."

"We'll leave the front door unlocked. Just let her in. It'll be fun for the girls to have a sleepover. Good night, Mickey."

"Good night, Treat. I'll call you tomorrow."

"You'd better."

Treat fell asleep with a smile on her face. All was well in her world.

Chapter Nine

Treat got up early the next morning feeling like a new woman. She fixed herself a cup of tea. She and Bella sat on the stairs near the front door to wait for Mickey and Lucy. When she heard Mickey's car pull up, she stepped outside. Mickey and Lucy got out of the car. Lucy ran to Bella, and they began playing together. Mickey walked up to Treat and took her in her arms.

"You feel so good. What are you doing up so early?"

"To see you, of course."

"Sweetie, I've got to go. Don't forget me while I'm gone, okay?"

"How could I?"

Treat watched Mickey drive off her property. She wasn't sure what she was feeling—elation, caution, wonderment, lust—all rolled into one confused mass sitting in the center of her chest.

Treat called the dogs to her and returned to the house. Treat worked out in her gym for an hour, and felt better for it. She took a shower and joined Denis in the kitchen for breakfast.

"I'm not sure how to break this to you," Denis said, pausing for dramatic effect. "Your dog cloned herself during the night. I'm sure when I went to bed we only had Bella. This morning, I found Bella and her clone waiting for me."

Treat laughed. "Mickey dropped Lucy off on her way out of town, silly."

"We need to talk before this thing with Mickey goes too much further, girlfriend."

"What thing? Why?"

"Let me fix breakfast and then we'll talk."

"We can talk while you fix breakfast."

"Okay." Denis gathered the fixings for French toast and began his preparations.

"What's going on, Denis. What do you know?"

"It's what I don't know that's bothering me."

"All right. What don't you know?"

"I Googled Mickey the other night."

"Why?"

"Mostly out of curiosity. Then I wondered what I would find if I Googled you, so I did. The first thing that popped up on you was the *Forbes* magazine article on the world's richest women, and there you were. According to them, you're a very, very wealthy woman. And because of that, you're never going to be footloose and fancy free. But you already knew that. I've told you this before, but now it's no longer an option, it's a necessity. I'm interviewing security firms."

"Have you forgotten, I used to own a security firm?"

"No, I haven't forgotten. It's not your company's security I'm worried about. It's your security I'm worried about."

"My security? Why are you bothered about that? I've not been threatened."

She looked at Denis, who couldn't meet her eyes. "Denis, what's going on?"

"Maybe I've been watching too many films. I thought that because you've been proclaimed the tenth richest woman in the world, we may want to protect you from idiots who may kidnap you for the ransom they know you can afford or from someone pretending to be someone they're not in order to get close to you. Besides, if we wait until you're threatened, it's too late to hire protection."

"Isn't that a tad paranoid? Look, I know there's something else going on, but I'm willing to talk about it later. Tell me about Mickey."

"That's what got me worried. Mickey doesn't exist."

Treat stood up and went to the window. She stared out the window while her mind processed what Denis had told her. This can't be true. The implications of why Mickey didn't exist as Mickey Heiden were enormous.

"What are the chances, in this day and age, that a person who is Googled won't turn up at least one hit?" Denis asked.

"Slim, very slim."

"When I Googled Mickey and nothing came back, I dug a little deeper. Still nothing. So I called John Stacy at D and T. He owes me a favor, so I asked him to do an in-depth search on Mickey. He called while you were in the shower. He hasn't turned up anything either. That intrigues him, and he's going to dig deeper."

Treat returned to her chair. *Clearly, Mickey's been lying to me about herself. But why? What's she hiding?*

"Dammit all to hell!" she said, slamming her hand down on the table in frustration and disappointment. "Let me know what you guys find. I want to know regardless of whether it's good or bad, understood?"

"Understood. I'm sorry, Treat. I know you care for her."

Treat's elated mood crashed down around her ankles like a helium balloon with a pinprick in it. Mickey hadn't been honest with her, that was certain. She thought of a dozen reasons why she might not exist and why she wouldn't tell Treat about who she really was. Maybe she was a criminal and in hiding. Maybe she was hiding from a killer. Maybe she was in a witness protection program. Maybe she was hiding from someone she owed money to. *Maybe. Maybe. Maybe. Maybe you've been watching too many movies with Denis because now you're paranoid, too.* She continued to range over a host of possibilities before she stopped herself. She could, and would, drive herself crazy trying to figure out why there was no record of Mickey. She could also drive herself crazy not trying to figure out what the hell was going on.

Treat wondered what Mickey would say if she asked her who she really was. She didn't have a number for her in Montpelier. She did, however, have her cell phone number.

"Denis? I really appreciate what you're doing, boyfriend. Thanks for having my back."

"Always."

"We need to find out where Mickey is. I brought some equipment with me, did you?"

"Yeah. You know I don't like to be too far away from my toys."

"Good. Let's get set up in my office."

"Are you thinking she's not in Montpelier? Why would you think that?" Denis asked.

"I don't think that. It's just that all this talk of intrigue and Mickey not existing has me thinking. When I say this stuff out loud, I sound as paranoid as you do when you talk about it."

"I'm not accusing Mickey of anything—one way or another. I'm just very, very curious how someone cannot exist."

The phone rang, and Denis answered it. He did a lot of "uh-huhs" before he finally hung up.

"That was John," Denis told her. "It appears Mickey Heiden really does not exist. He found no record of her in any of the databases, with the exception of a Mickey Heiden who died in 1945 in Texas. He says he can hack into a couple of the government databases if we want him to, but it will take much longer."

"Tell him no. I want to talk to Mickey first."

"You need to be careful, Treat. She's obviously not who she says she is, and we're not sure how far she'll go to protect her identity. Or if she's alone in this whatever it is."

"Before we go completely nuts over this and get so paranoid we don't trust anyone, I'll talk to her and see what she says. If we don't believe her, then we'll discuss our next step."

"I'm not sure that's a good idea."

"Why not? Mickey doesn't know we know she's not who she says she is, so I'm no threat to her."

"Be careful anyway. Okay?"

"Yeah, yeah. Talk to me about personal security. Are you entirely sure it's necessary?"

"Let's see. You just made the *Forbes* list, and yet you live alone in a house in the middle of fucking nowhere. So yeah, I think we need to talk about it."

"I want to sit in on any interviews you do. If we do hire someone, I don't want it to be some machismo testosterone-driven asshole. And I don't want my freedom curtailed."

"We'll talk details after we talk to the security firms."

"Do you know where the puppies are?" Treat asked, standing up.

"I don't have a clue. But they're quiet. That does not bode well for us humans."

"Help me find them. I'm sure they need to go outside. Do you want to go for a drive later?"

"Sure. Where are we driving to?"

"Nowhere in particular."

"Uh-huh," Denis said skeptically.

They found the puppies asleep in the sun on the living room floor. She bent down and gently woke them. Her heart melted yet again when they looked up at her with complete trust and love.

The few things Treat had arranged to be shipped from California arrived as Treat and Denis were getting ready to leave the house. Treat and Denis spent the rest of the morning unpacking boxes and putting things away. She was particularly glad to see her clothes. She was tired of wearing the same few pieces of clothing she'd brought with her.

After lunch, Treat and Denis decided to go for their drive. They hadn't had time to explore their environs, and only really knew the road from Guilford to Brattleboro. The surrounding countryside remained a mystery. They took Denis's rental car because Treat wanted to think and couldn't if she was driving.

Treat had Denis make a couple of turns. They ended up on Mickey's road. As they drove past her house, Mickey's truck was in the driveway.

"Is that Mickey's house?" Denis wanted to know.

"Yes, it is. That's her truck."

"Great."

"I wish I could agree. Turn around as soon as you can. I don't want her to see us up here."

"She won't recognize this car."

"It's been in the driveway the last couple of times she's come to visit. As an artist, I suspect she's observant enough to make a note of at least the color of the car, if not the make and model. Let's just get the hell off her road."

As they drove past Mickey's house a second time, Mickey was standing out on the deck with her back to the road, and another woman stood in front of her.

"Ouch," Denis commented.

"I guess if you're going to spy on people, you're bound to see a few things you'd rather not."

They drove around the countryside without a destination. They only spoke when one or the other saw something intriguing. As dusk turned to evening, they started back to the house because they were hungry and could no longer see anything from the road.

"Isn't it time you turn this car back to Avis?" Treat asked.

"Great minds think alike. I don't believe we need two cars. We'll take it back tomorrow."

As they pulled into their driveway, Treat's heart began to race. Mickey was leaning against her truck with her long legs crossed at the ankles. "Damn," Treat whispered.

Treat got out of the car and walked toward Mickey. "Hey," Treat said.

Mickey ran her eyes over her. Watching Mickey look at her caused her blood to run hot with lust. She wanted nothing more than to grab Mickey's hand and drag her upstairs to her new bed and properly initiate it.

Mickey drew Treat into an embrace and held her without saying anything.

"My God, you feel fantastic, Treat."

Too many questions were running through Treat's mind to know how to respond to Mickey. Her body was telling her one thing, her heart was inclined to agree, but her mind was reminding the others they didn't know who this woman was.

"Mickey, what are you doing back in town? I thought you had to be in Montpelier for a few days."

"I couldn't stop thinking about you. I got what I needed from them and told them I could only work in my own studio."

"You played the artistic diva card?"

"Only partially. I do work better in my own studio, but they didn't know I wanted to see you more than I wanted their job. Is that crazy?"

"Yes, it is, girlfriend. Come on in. I've got two girls who can't wait to see you."

"And you? Did you miss me?"

Treat laughed and said, "Like the devil."

Treat took Mickey's hand, and they walked into the house.

Denis came out of the kitchen and said, "Mickey. Welcome back."

"Thank you. We're looking for the girls."

"I only this second let them out back."

"Mickey, why don't you go out there, I'll be there in a minute," Treat said.

Once Mickey was outside, Treat whispered to Denis, "Call the Verdant Gallery in Montpelier and find out if she was there today and/or if she was given a commission by them."

"Will do. Did she say why she's back?"

"She missed me."

"I just bet she did," Denis said, sarcastically.

Later, Treat, Mickey, and Denis had dinner in the kitchen. After helping Denis clear the dishes, the two women, with the two puppies following them, headed out to the patio. They settled in chairs while the puppies raced around chasing ghosts and each other.

"Treat…"

"Mickey…"

They laughed. "You first," Mickey said.

"All right. I've been thinking. It bothers me I know nothing about you. You've very deftly turn any discussion away from yourself. I need to find out more."

"Like what?"

"Don't play these games with me, Mickey."

"I'm sorry. Old habits die hard, very hard."

"Nevertheless, I need to know more about you."

"I don't know where to begin. By the way, where were you and Denis? I thought I saw his rental car on my road earlier."

"Mickey…"

"Sorry. I don't know where to begin."

"How about beginning with where you really were before you came to Guilford."

"How do you know I've been anywhere else? Not all of us are non-natives, you know."

Treat abruptly stood up, startling the puppies and Mickey. She was tired of Mickey's evasions. Mickey had already told her she'd moved to Vermont from DC. Why be evasive about that now?

"I will not play these games with you."

"I'm not playing games."

"Yes, you are. If you don't want to share your past, that's your business. If that's your choice, however, I don't have to accept it. And I don't. It's time for you to leave."

"You cannot be serious."

"Yes, I can, and I am. Others may find your mysterious persona alluring, but I don't."

"Treat…"

Treat was already heading for the door. For a minute, the puppies were confused. Bella headed after Treat at a run while Lucy stayed with Mickey.

As she walked through the kitchen, she told Denis, "Mickey's leaving. I'll be in my office. Come in when she's gone."

Denis saw Mickey out of the house. Mickey paused before going down the steps. "Do you know what this is all about, Denis?"

"No. Why don't you tell me what happened."

Mickey filled him in on her short conversation with Treat.

"I think you've met your match, Mickey. Treat is as private as they come. She won't betray your confidences, and you can trust her implicitly. I doubt, though, she's willing to go down a one-way street with you. You can't expect her to share her heart with you while you clam up every time she tries to get to know you better."

Mickey turned and walked to her truck without another word. She helped Lucy into the cab before getting in.

Treat heard the truck start and knew there was an excellent chance Mickey was driving out of her life. She felt such a loss she wanted to cry.

When Denis entered Treat's office, he found her staring out the windows into the blackness outside as she had so many nights in California after Chloe died. He walked to her side and stood silently waiting for her to stop her memories and come back to him.

"Did you call the gallery?"

"Yes. They were just closing, but the owner was more than happy to talk to me when I told her who I worked for. She had seen the article in *Forbes*. She told me she knew who Mickey was—a talented new sculptor who worked in wood—but she had not commissioned a piece by her. She wants you to know that if you want a piece of Mickey's work, you need only ask her and the gallery will provide it."

"Thanks for doing that for me, Denis. What the hell do you think is going on?"

"I haven't a clue. It's too weird for me to get my head around. Have you asked her?"

"Not in so many words, but yes. She tries to change the subject or simply evades the questions."

"What are you going to do?" Denis asked.

"I don't know. I find myself thinking about her all the time. She's so talented, so beautiful..." Treat trailed off.

"And so sexy."

Treat laughed and said, "Yes, and so very, very sexy. I almost skipped dinner tonight to drag her upstairs. I wish now I had. I'm sure the reality of making love with her is so much better than my fantasies."

"Then call her. Or better yet, go over to her house."

"I can't."

"Why not?"

"Because, Denis, what if she has a woman with her? Then what would I do?"

"Drive away and come home."

"No. I'll survive. I've survived this long without Mickey Heiden, I can survive without her for the rest of my life."

"Are you sure?"

"No. Yes. Maybe."

It was Denis's turn to laugh. "I love it when you're decisive, Treat."

CHAPTER TEN

A month later, Treat was in the backyard playing ball with Bella when she saw Denis standing at the kitchen window watching. Bella was nearly inexhaustible when it came to chasing her ball. Long after Treat lost interest in the game, Bella was begging for more. Now Treat headed for the house and her morning tea, while Bella wanted one last throw. Bella stood looking so disappointed, but Treat studiously ignored her big brown eyes and headed for the house.

"Good morning," Treat said to Denis when she entered the kitchen. "I wonder if I can buy one of those machines that tosses baseballs or tennis balls at people. If we had one of those, I'd only need to turn it on and Bella could chase balls until she was exhausted."

"I'm sure you can buy one. The cost is probably prohibitive, though. I wonder if Bella would understand the concept of earning the money to put one of those machines in the backyard."

"Bella's a smart girl and can learn anything except when to quit."

"You seem up this morning," Denis said.

"I am. I'm thinking of leaving Vermont."

"What? I thought you loved it here."

"I do. But…"

"But she's here, too?"

"Something like that."

"Want breakfast?"

"No. Tea is enough."

After Denis finished his coffee, he headed into town to do the grocery shopping. Treat went to the living room and sat in her rocker, reading. She did not notice time passing and was surprised when Denis walked in announcing that luncheon was served in the kitchen.

After lunch, Treat stood up and stretched out her tightly bunched muscles. She followed Denis out to the patio. Bella was already there sunbathing. Denis told Treat where he had gone that morning and what he had bought. He gave her a written menu for the week asking her to make any changes she wanted.

"I think the days we can sit out here are about over. It's getting colder by the day," Denis said.

"I wonder when the first snow will come our way?"

"Hopefully in February with the last in March?"

Treat laughed. "Keep dreaming, Den."

"Guess who I ran into at the Co-Op?" The Co-Op was Brattleboro's food cooperative.

"I have no idea. Anybody I know?"

"Mickey."

Treat felt her stomach lurch at the mention of Mickey's name.

"And?" she asked casually, or at least she hoped it sounded casual.

"And nothing. We chatted awhile over a really good cup of coffee in the café and then we parted company."

"How did she look?"

"She looked stunning. Sexy. She turned so many heads,

it's hard to tell the straights from the gays when she's in the room."

Treat laughed. Having been at the dance at the River View with Mickey, she knew exactly what Denis meant. She had wondered if the entire town was lesbian until she realized everyone, male and female, turned and watched Mickey Heiden. No wonder the woman had so much bedroom action.

"Treat, she asked how you were doing."

"Please tell me you did not tell her I was pining over her."

"No, of course not. I told her you were doing wonderfully well, and you were thinking of leaving the area."

"What did she say?"

"Nothing. She changed the subject."

"She is very good at that, isn't she?"

"Very adroit at it, I would say. I bet it was very frustrating for you trying to have a conversation with her about herself."

"So frustrating that I haven't seen her in over a month. In any case, though, I'm pretty sure she hasn't let any grass grow under her feet."

"Why would she? You tossed her out of your life, Treat."

"Yes, I did."

"Regrets?"

"No. Yes. I still wish I knew what she was hiding or hiding from."

"Would knowing make a difference?"

"I think it might."

CHAPTER ELEVEN

Treat spent the afternoon working. As she left her office, she was surprised to hear Denis in the kitchen. Surely it was not dinnertime. Before she could reach the kitchen, she heard a car pull up in front of the house.

As she stepped out the front door, her first reaction was to turn around and go back inside. Mickey was coming to a skidding stop. She flung open the door of her truck, stepped out followed by Lucy, and strode toward Treat.

"You cannot leave."

"I can and will."

"No, you can't."

"All right. Tell me why you think you can tell me I can't leave."

Mickey paused. "Because."

"That's your reason? Because."

"Yes. No. It's complicated."

"Not for me it's not."

"Treat, please. Cut me some slack here. I don't want you to leave."

The two women had squared off like two pugilists in a ring. Treat's anger was on the rise. Mickey's gray eyes had turned the color of an angry sky on a summer's day when a thunderstorm was moving in.

"I don't care what you want, Mickey. You don't have the right to even ask me not to go. Damn it, you can't even give me a reason to stay. Oh, wait. Your reason is 'because.' That's *very* persuasive."

"Your sarcasm isn't helping any, Treat."

"Your secretiveness is killing this."

"This what?"

"Whatever was developing between us."

"Why does it matter who or what I may have been before I met you?"

"What you were before you met me makes you who you are today. And while we're on the subject of who you were, I don't give a damn who you fucked before I met you, but I do care who you fuck now."

Oh, shit, Treat! she admonished herself. *Did you really have to go there?* Treat couldn't tell if Mickey was surprised at her statement. It was, however, obvious they were both becoming angrier by the second. Treat told herself, *it doesn't matter, there can't possibly be anything between us now.* Treat knew if they didn't stop, more things were going to be said that should not be said, but she was powerless to stop herself. *Don't take this personally. It's not about you. It's all about her. Take a step back, Treat, and breathe.* But she didn't.

"It's none of your damn business who I fuck. Period," Mickey said.

❖

As soon as those words left her mouth, Mickey knew three things for certain. One was she'd gone too far. Two, it wasn't true; she wanted it to be Treat's business. And three, she loved the idea Treat cared enough to be jealous.

❖

Treat was surprised at how rapidly things between them had gotten out of control. Treat hadn't realized how angry she was with Mickey for having been in the arms of another woman. Nor had she known she could be jealous. Chloe had never given her any reason to be even remotely jealous, and she had certainly never caught Chloe in the arms of another woman. With a calm that belied the turmoil inside, Treat said, "You're absolutely right. It is not any of my business. Not now. Not ever."

As Treat turned to go back inside, Mickey closed the space between them, putting her hand on Treat's shoulder.

"Treat, wait."

"For what, Mickey? What should I wait for?"

"I want to say the things I came here to say. And I want you to listen."

"I think we just said everything we need to say, Mickey." Treat tried to pull away, but Mickey kept her hand on her shoulder.

"Take your hand off me," Treat said with ice lacing her voice.

Mickey complied. "I haven't told you how you affect me, Treat. I haven't told you I can't sleep at night because I ache for you. I haven't told you I could easily fall in love with you. I haven't told you who I am. I haven't told you I've been waiting for someone like you for a long time. I haven't told you how scared I am right this minute I'm about to lose you. I'm scared if I feel this way now, how am I going to feel once we've spent time together and we've made love? I'm scared, Treat."

Treat hoped Mickey was telling the truth. What she said had the ring of honesty to it. Equally important, it felt like it had been wrung out of Mickey. It had taken so much courage for Mickey to speak. Treat felt her anger melt away. She also saw a much deeper emotion in Mickey's eyes, but what it was she wasn't quite sure. Fear? What could Mickey be so afraid of?

"Mickey," was all Treat could manage to say.

You need to walk away now because Mickey is nothing but trouble. There's something not right about her. There's something big she's hiding from you. Her heart and body, though, kept telling her to stay, to see what time would bring. Against her better judgment, she remained.

When Treat turned to put her hand on Mickey's sternum, Mickey exhaled the breath she'd been holding.

"Treat, I will never knowingly hurt you."

"Don't say that, Mickey. Keeping a part of you from me and lying to me is hurting me. I'm trying to figure out if I'm willing to endure that hurt in order to be with you. I don't know. Maybe—at least for now. When it becomes too much for me to bear, I will leave."

"No, don't say you'll leave me, Treat. Don't say that. I will tell you what I can now and the rest will come later. I promise."

Treat smiled at the promise wondering how much truth was there and how much was Mickey wanting it to be true but knowing it wasn't.

"Why don't we go out back? The girls are probably out there sunning themselves. I know Denis made some fresh lemonade earlier."

"The really tart kind like you like or the sweeter kind the rest of the world can tolerate?"

"My kind, if he knows what's good for him," Treat said with a smile.

Mickey took Treat's hand and brought it to her lips, softly kissing Treat's palm. The touch of Mickey's lips sent an immediate message to Treat's core. She wasn't sure, but thought maybe she groaned at the touch, and when she looked at Mickey, she was sure she had moaned out loud because there was the slightest smile on her lips.

"Treat, I'd like nothing better than to drop down and do it right here in the grass. However, I want our first time to be in a bed where I can make love to you slowly and for hours."

"Oh my," was all Treat could manage.

Mickey started toward the back of the house, but Treat held her back. "Are you sure it has to be in a bed? Won't a bed of grass be just as good?"

"Yes, a bed of grass would be good, but I don't think we could do it for hours here on your front lawn without at least Denis coming to find us. We certainly wouldn't want to scandalize the natives should one of them venture up your driveway," Mickey told her with a laugh.

"All right, all right. Damn! Who knew you would be so logical."

The girls spied them as they turned the corner of the house and galumphed their way over to them. Both puppies promptly brought tennis balls to be thrown.

"You do know they will not let you stop throwing the balls for a long time. Is there something you're trying to avoid?"

"No. I just want you to keep thinking about what I'll be doing to you later. I want you to be so hot that when I touch you, you'll be begging to come."

"You think that will take a while? I've got news for you. I'm already wet. You think about that for a while."

Treat turned and headed for the kitchen to get lemonade for them. As she entered the kitchen, Denis asked, "Did you guys make up?"

"Yes. She'll be staying the night, I think."

"Well, good. I've got a date, and I don't think I'll be home. Let's have an early dinner, shall we? I don't have to leave until eight, so we'll have dinner at six thirty."

"You have a date? Where did you meet him? What does he look like? Give details."

"You know I don't kiss and tell."

"You've already kissed? I knew you were fast, but this is a record even for you."

"No, we haven't kissed."

"What's the problem? You've always given me too much information in the past. What's going on, Denis?"

"I don't know myself. He's not even my type."

"You have a type? I didn't know that."

"Very funny."

"So…"

"So nothing."

"Don't make me hurt you, Den. Where's he from?"

"Brattleboro."

"Really? You're going to date a hick?"

"Desperate times call for desperate measures. Don't rub my nose in my previously haughty attitude."

"What's he do for a living?"

"He's a lawyer."

Treat was surprised. Denis hated lawyers with a passion. He had been a practicing attorney for several years before walking away from a lucrative practice to become Treat's housekeeper.

"I'm stunned into silence."

"That's all I'm going to tell you now. Well, except he's gorgeous in an offbeat sort of way."

"Okay. I can live with that. At least bring him home some evening to meet your family."

"I will. Although it won't be any time real soon."

"Okay. Come join Mickey and me and the puppies when you can."

Denis had already turned back to his dinner preparations and had put the ear buds to his iPod in his ears, effectively tuning out the world.

CHAPTER TWELVE

When Treat returned to the patio, Mickey was still tossing balls, and the puppies were still chasing them. When Bella saw Treat, she dropped her ball and came running to her. Treat set their drinks on the table between two lounge chairs and sat down. Bella crawled onto the chair and nestled between Treat's legs.

"This is embarrassing. How can I be jealous of a puppy? How come I don't get to do that?" Mickey asked in a mock petulant voice.

"Because she was more than just talk."

Mickey chortled. "No fair, I told you we could drop down in the grass if you really wanted to."

"You did no such thing, lady. You were determined to tease me."

"You don't know the meaning of the word yet."

"Really?" Treat asked raising an eyebrow. "By the way, Denis has a date tonight, so we'll have the house to ourselves."

"Who's he seeing?"

"I don't know. He wasn't very forthcoming. He did say the guy is a lawyer."

"I wonder which one. I wasn't aware we had any gay lawyers in town. Gay everything else, but no lawyers."

"He said the guy is from Brattleboro, so I'd say you have at least one."

"I wonder if I can get Denis to tell me his name?"

Treat, of course, wondered why she'd be concerned about a gay lawyer. *Dammit, I wish she'd just tell me what the hell is going on.*

As the afternoon passed, the two women sat and talked quietly. The puppies had settled down with their respective mistresses, and occasionally one would dash into the yard, followed by the other. They would play for a while and then return to take another nap. It got cooler with each passing hour. By four thirty, the sun was setting, and Treat decided it was too cold to be sitting outside. She moved them into the living room and ran upstairs to grab a sweater. When she returned, Mickey had gotten a sweater from her truck.

Dinner was delicious, but it was interminably long even though they were at the table for only an hour. Mickey got Denis to tell her the name of the attorney he was seeing and then changed the subject. Every time she looked at Mickey, Mickey would let her eyes drop to Treat's breasts, then return her eyes to meet Treat's. She smiled when Treat squirmed in her chair.

"Is there a problem, Treat?" Denis wanted to know.

"What do you mean?" Treat asked.

"Well, you seem uncomfortable. You're squirming."

"I'm not squirming," Treat announced, embarrassed to tell Denis Mickey was making her so hot she couldn't sit still.

After dinner, Denis served them coffee and tea in the living room despite Treat's protests they could fend for themselves. He smiled and then left them to get ready for his date. Treat and Mickey sat on opposite ends of the couch facing one another. Treat had run out of small talk. The only talking she wanted to do was with her body and her hands. Mickey apparently wasn't having the same problem concentrating. Treat thought she was enjoying her discomfort all too much.

When Mickey stretched out and put her stockinged foot hard against the V between Treat's legs, Treat gasped. Slowly, Mickey pressed harder and backed off, pressed harder and backed off. Treat put her hand on Mickey's foot to stop the exquisite pressure. "If you don't stop that right now, I'm going to come."

"That's okay with me. I'd love to watch you come."

"You really do like to tease, don't you?"

"It's not teasing, Treat. It's a promise of things to come."

Denis said from the door, "I'll just be going now. You two enjoy yourselves."

No sooner had the door closed on Denis than Mickey started crawling toward Treat without taking her eyes off her. She put a hand on the couch on either side of Treat and leaned in to kiss her. It was so unexpectedly tender Treat felt something melt within her. When Mickey deepened her kiss, Treat arched, trying to make contact with Mickey, but Mickey was careful to keep her body away. Treat was fully aroused and needed to pull Mickey down on her, but Mickey was up and away from her so fast Treat barely saw her move.

"I think I'll be going home, Treat," Mickey said with a sensuous smile.

"Mickey Heiden, if you try to leave, I will, so help me God, tackle you and have my way with you where you land."

"I do believe you're threatening me."

"I am indeed."

"I think I'd like to see you try to tackle me."

"Mickey. Please."

"Please what?"

"Please make love to me."

"Anytime, anywhere."

CHAPTER THIRTEEN

Treat took Mickey's hand and led her to the stairs where she let go of Mickey's hand and started up the stairs to her bedroom. Once in the bedroom, Treat thought Mickey became shy and unsure of herself as she stood watching Treat dimming the lights in the room. When she was through, Treat walked up to Mickey and lifted her sweater over her head. Then she began slowly unbuttoning her shirt while maintaining eye contact. By the time she reached Mickey's belt buckle, Mickey's breathing was heavier, and her gray eyes had darkened. She didn't remove the shirt. Instead, she pulled it down tight over Mickey's nipples, creating a tautness that accentuated their hardness.

Treat moved behind Mickey and slowly pulled her shirt from her slacks, slid it off her shoulders, and let it drop to the floor. Next, she unsnapped Mickey's bra and kissed the nape of Mickey's neck as she moved her hands down Mickey's back, but stopping short of her ass. She caressed her way back to Mickey's shoulders. Mickey leaned against Treat.

Treat moved to stand in front of Mickey once more. She put her hand between Mickey's breasts and felt Mickey's heart pounding, then brushed her hand over Mickey's left breast and heard her moan. She moved her hands down to Mickey's belt and back up her torso.

Mickey tried unsuccessfully to suppress a moan as Treat repeated the movement over her breasts.

Treat kissed Mickey on the lips softly and then ran her tongue over Mickey's parted lips. She explored those lips with her tongue and slid it inside slowly. Mickey stepped closer to Treat so their bodies were touching at as many points as possible.

Treat took a step away from Mickey. "Come with me," Treat whispered huskily as she backed toward the bed. As she felt the bed behind her knees, Treat sat down and drew Mickey between her legs.

She began unbuckling Mickey's belt. She moved the zipper of Mickey's slacks down as slowly as she was able. Mickey moaned as the zipper reached the end of its track. Treat started sliding Mickey's slacks down her slim hips. As the slacks slipped to the floor, Treat could feel the heat emanating from Mickey.

Treat allowed Mickey to kick her slacks away before she started to remove Mickey's silk boxers. After Mickey kicked the boxers away, Treat began placing soft kisses at Mickey's navel and moved slowly downward one kiss at a time. She also moved her hands up Mickey's legs, and her kisses and hands reached Mickey's heat at the same time.

Mickey's breath was ragged, and she said, hoarsely, "Treat, I can't stand up anymore."

"So?"

"Uh, I need to lie down, I think."

Treat backed Mickey up a step and stood in front of her, kissing her deeply. She turned them around, at the same time moving Mickey toward the bed. Mickey was trying to unbutton Treat's shirt, but her hands had turned to putty, and she wasn't making much progress. Treat gently pushed her down on the bed and stepped away.

Treat began removing her own clothing, teasing Mickey with the deliberate unbuttoning of each button, and then removing her shirt to reveal nothing beneath but bare skin. Mickey gasped but didn't try to put her hands on Treat. Treat removed her slacks in slow motion, reveling in watching Mickey being mesmerized by each movement.

When Treat was standing naked, Mickey moved back onto the bed, drawing Treat with her. Treat kissed her way up Mickey's body, starting with the wetness between her legs and ending with a heart-stopping kiss on her mouth. Mickey raised her knee and Treat straddled it. She glided up and down Mickey's thigh as she sucked gently on Mickey's breasts. She took a nipple into her mouth and sucked as she moved her tongue across the erect nipple. Both women were breathing hard, wanting more.

"Treat, please," Mickey whispered.

"Please what?"

"Please let me come."

"In a minute. I want to taste you first."

Mickey moaned, not sure she could wait another second, much less a minute. As Mickey lowered her leg, Treat slid down the length of Mickey's body, trailing a hand behind her kisses. Treat knew she needed only to touch her lightly and she would come hard.

Treat reached the soft dampness of Mickey's heat and moved her hand to Mickey's thigh, feeling her own wetness there. She moved her hand up the inside of Mickey's thigh, feeling her arch in anticipation of Treat entering her. Treat removed her hand and blew warm air on Mickey's swollen clit.

Treat moved her tongue between Mickey's lips and lightly

stroked her. She also ran her hand up between Mickey's legs and inserted one finger and then a second finger inside Mickey. As she began to lightly suck on Mickey's clitoris, she felt the beginnings of Mickey's orgasm tightening around her fingers. As Mickey came, Treat heard her cry out.

Treat waited until the spasms lessened before slowly sliding out of Mickey. She moved up Mickey's body and covered Mickey with her own body, protecting her while she was so vulnerable. When at last Mickey stilled, Treat rolled off her but stayed close. She raised up on one elbow and put her hand on Mickey's cheek, surprised when she felt tears.

"Mickey, what's wrong?" she asked softly. "Did I hurt you?"

"No, no. You didn't hurt me."

"Then why the tears, baby?"

Mickey smiled at the word "baby."

"It's been so long, Treat."

"What's been so long?"

"It's been so long since I've been with a woman. So long since I've wanted to be with anyone. So long since I've let anyone touch me. So long since anyone called me 'baby.'"

Treat couldn't quite hide her surprise at Mickey's confession.

"How is that possible? You're beautiful, sexy, and intelligent. What more could a woman want from you?"

"Oh, I've had plenty of offers, but no one appealed to me until I saw you leaning against your car watching me."

"Why, Mickey?"

"It's a long story, and I will tell you. First, though, I want to make love to you. I want to feel what it's like to be inside you, to smell you, to taste you. To watch you come."

"Oh, Mickey," was all Treat could manage as she felt Mickey's hands slide down her body.

With each kiss and each caress, Treat became more aroused than the moment before. Just when she thought Mickey's kisses and caresses would make her come, Mickey slid her fingers inside her. Treat orgasmed so deeply and hard she thought her very cells were exploding.

After her wits returned to their rightful place, she heard Mickey whisper in her ear, "Roll over, love."

Treat rolled over onto her stomach. She felt Mickey move over her body and kiss the nape of her neck. Mickey slowly kissed her way from her neck to her shoulder blades. "Spread your, legs, baby." Treat spread her legs and felt Mickey slide between them as she continued kissing her way down her back. When Mickey reached the small of Treat's back, Treat felt Mickey's hands moving over her ass and responded by pushing into Mickey's hands. Mickey continued to move her hands from Treat's thighs to her knees. Mickey's mouth followed her hand across Treat's ass and down her left thigh. Mickey moved her hands to the inside of Treat's thighs and moved them slowly upward. When she reached the apex of Treat's legs, she lightly touched the glistening wetness there. Treat wanted, no, needed Mickey to touch her, but Mickey moved on without going where Treat wanted her to be. Treat moaned, silently begging Mickey to enter her. When Mickey put two fingers inside and caressed her ass with her other hand, Treat again exploded.

As she recovered, Treat rolled over and allowed herself to be pulled into the safety of Mickey's strong arms. Mickey held her tightly.

When Treat awoke, she reached for Mickey but found the bed empty. "Mickey?" Her mind told her Mickey had left.

"Over here." Mickey's wonderfully husky voice came out of the darkness near the windows. "Join me and bring the bedspread."

Treat picked up the bedspread from where it had slid off the bed. She found Mickey standing in front of the windows. Mickey took the bedspread from her.

"Close your eyes," Mickey said as she took Treat's hand and guided her to stand in front of her.

Mickey swirled the bedspread around her shoulders and enfolded Treat into the cocoon she'd created. Treat could feel the coolness of Mickey's body against her back and wondered how long she'd been standing in front of the window.

"Open your eyes."

"It's snowing!" Treat exclaimed as she watched the large flakes drift toward the ground. Already there was a light dusting of snow on the meadow, and it was beginning to accumulate in the trees of the woods. Adding to the beauty of the snowfall was a full moon that illuminated the landscape and turned it into a fairy-tale scene.

"Beautiful, isn't it? I'm going to open the window, and I want you to listen to the sound of snow falling."

After Mickey opened the window, Treat strained to hear something, anything. All she heard was silence. The sound of falling snow was silence. It was a magical moment. When Mother Nature paused to admire her handiwork, there was only silence.

Treat felt Mickey shiver behind her. She closed the window and led Mickey back to bed. After they pulled the covers over themselves, Treat said, "Thank you for sharing."

"You're welcome. I love the first snow of the season."

Treat could not have imagined a more perfect ending to the day than sharing an enchanted moment with Mickey.

CHAPTER FOURTEEN

Treat was the first to wake. She was on her side snuggled against Mickey's back. Her arm was thrown possessively over the other woman's waist. Mickey whimpered and started to roll over. Treat scooted backward to get out of her way. Mickey lay on her back, still asleep.

Treat's breath caught in her throat as she watched her lover. Mickey asleep was a different woman. The intensity was gone—there was a softness about her that was not present when she was awake. Treat let her eyes roam over Mickey's body. She took in all the angles and planes. Her eyes paused on a faint scar on Mickey's face running from near the outside corner of her left eye down to the jawline. She couldn't imagine how it had happened or what had caused it. Her eyes continued down Mickey's body, enjoying the taut body. She gasped when she got to Mickey's left thigh—running nearly ten inches down Mickey's thigh toward her knee was a scar, still angrily red and looking painful.

Treat ran her hand lightly over Mickey's abdomen and watched the muscles quiver. Mickey stirred and opened her eyes. This morning they were the palest shade of gray.

"Hey there," Mickey said sleepily.

"You okay?" Treat asked hesitantly.

"Don't know for sure, but I think I'm more than okay."

"I hope I didn't hurt you last night, Mickey," Treat told her as she slid her hand down Mickey's rippling stomach to her thigh and gently down the length of the scar.

Mickey smiled. "No. You didn't hurt me. Everything you did made me feel wonderful. I hope I made you feel the same."

"Oh, yeah. You should have no doubt of that, lady."

"I'm glad. Uh, if you keep doing that, I'm going to have to jump your bones."

"Doing what?" Treat asked innocently.

"As I recall, you do like to tease, don't you?"

"Yes, I do. Complaints?"

"None. Absolutely no complaints."

"Good. I'm glad we got that settled," Treat told her as she languidly moved her hand up Mickey's thigh and cupped her. She smiled at Mickey's gasp but held her hand very still, sensing Mickey would come if she moved again. Treat wanted to tease her a lot longer.

Mickey opened her eyes again and looked at Treat. Treat saw her eyes had changed color to the dusky gray of arousal. She moved her hand slightly and felt Mickey tense.

"Treat. Please be inside me."

"Mickey, I want to make you come, truly I do, but I think it's too soon."

"You are such a tease. Trust me, it's not too soon."

"Well, darling, you're not even breathing hard yet."

She leaned over and gently took Mickey's nipple between her lips and sucked lightly. At the same time, she moved her hand so she could slip two fingers inside Mickey while keeping her thumb on Mickey's clitoris. She began running her thumb up and down the bundle of nerve endings. Mickey arched.

"Deeper," Mickey managed to gasp out.

"Yes, dear," Treat told her as she moved deeper into

Mickey. She felt Mickey's orgasm building around her fingers. She increased the pressure on Mickey's nipple. She was rewarded by Mickey's moan of pleasure. She quickened the rhythm of her fingers and increased the pressure on Mickey's clit. She knew Mickey could not hold out very much longer and knew that she, too, would come from feeling Mickey on her hand and listening to Mickey's moans.

"I'm coming," Mickey gasped.

"I know, Mickey. Go ahead. I want to come with you."

Mickey tried to move so she could touch Treat, but Treat refused to let her.

"Mickey, I'm so aroused that when you come, I'll come."

With those words, Mickey threw her head back and cried out as her orgasm took control. Treat orgasmed when she heard Mickey's cry. They lay still, each trying to catch her breath and make her way back to the present.

"Do you have to be anywhere today?" Treat asked.

"No, and it's a good thing. I don't think I can stand, let alone walk," she said.

"Do you want to sleep?"

"No. What I want to do is look at you."

The two women changed positions, so Mickey was lying on her side, resting her head on the palm of her hand. Treat was on her back, totally relaxed. She watched as Mickey ran her eyes down the length of her torso, feeling a jolt when Mickey's eyes rested on her breasts and another when they rested on the wet triangle between her legs.

"You're very good at this," Mickey told her.

"So are you, sweetie. You didn't forget a thing during your period of celibacy."

"You are so beautiful, Treat. I have a hard time keeping my hands off you. When we're not together, I can only think about you and how soon I can be with you again."

"If that's true, why did it take you a month to come to me?"

"I was, and am, scared."

"Scared? You?"

"As I said, it's been a long time. Talk about performance anxiety!"

"Well, you certainly have no worries in that department. Is that all there is to being scared?"

"Not really. But it's the one I can most easily live with on a day-to-day basis."

"Will you tell me the whole reason you're scared?"

"Yes. Or at least I think I can."

Mickey was silent for so long that Treat almost said something.

"I'm trying so hard not to bolt right now. But you've made it very clear that if I want you in my life, I'm going to have to tell you my whole story. Since I've only discussed it with one other person, it's very hard for me to even begin. I'm afraid if I tell you, I'll be putting your life in danger. If I don't tell you, then I'll lose you. It's a terrible choice to have to make."

Treat kept silent. She stayed very still as well, not wanting to distract Mickey. She could feel the tension in Mickey's body, and she could almost feel the struggle raging within Mickey about whether to tell her the truth. Treat understood she was, for all practical purposes, a stranger to Mickey. Perhaps Mickey wasn't sure how she would react when she heard the truth of who she really was.

"I'll skip right to the chase. We can exchange childhood stories later. My name is not really Mickey Heiden. It's Jo Michael Vicenza. I am a colonel in the Marine Corps in the JAG—a prosecutor for the Judge Advocate General. I loved my job and I was good. My conviction rate was outstanding— perhaps too outstanding.

"One day, at the end of another successful conviction, as I was walking out of the courthouse, a man who looked vaguely familiar approached me. The cretin's name is Sheridan Blackhorn, a Marine I convicted for a string of assaults, rapes, and three murders committed at duty stations around the world. As he approached me, he pulled a gun from beneath his jacket. Apparently, someone jostled him just as he pulled the trigger, and his first shot grazed my cheek. There was no doubt in my mind he was going to kill me. I felt a hand on my back. I was pushed out of the way as he pulled the trigger a second time. His bullet missed me. A third shot rang out, and Blackhorn fell, but he wasn't dead. He managed to get a fourth shot off, and that one hit my leg. I looked at my leg and saw the blood pumping out and knew he had hit an artery, and I was going to die."

Mickey paused and took a deep breath, then continued, "Luckily for me, there was a doctor in the crowd, a witness in another trial. He saved my life. The woman who pushed me out of the way and took the kill shot meant for me died."

Tears rolled down Mickey's face as she told the story. She paused again and took another deep breath.

"The woman who died to save my life was my lover, Grace. We were supposed to meet at a restaurant for dinner to celebrate our fifteenth anniversary, but she wanted to surprise me and came to the courthouse instead. She wasn't even supposed to be there. If I had insisted she go in front of me out of the building, she'd still be alive. I didn't think I would recover from losing her. I've been living day to day, just putting one foot in front of the other." Mickey paused to catch her breath.

"I'm so sorry," Treat whispered.

Mickey resumed her story after a minute. "The wound on my thigh was very nasty mostly because the bullet ricocheted off a bone, nicked the femoral artery, and then severely damaged the muscle. The physical therapy was long and hard. That was only physical. The wound to my psyche was harder to heal. I was no longer interested in life. I was scared of my own shadow. A year after the attack, I was put into the Witness Protection Program, but that's a whole other story and best left for another time.

"Even before I was put in the Witness Protection Program, I wasn't living up to the Corps' standards for its lawyers. It was suggested by the Corps that perhaps I should take a medical retirement. But the Marine Corps was the only job I'd ever had, and I didn't want to retire. That was three years ago. The last surgery on my leg was two months before I met you.

"Grace is the reason I haven't been with another woman for so long. It's always felt like I was cheating on her. Until you."

Treat was stunned. She wasn't sure what she thought Mickey's story would be, but certainly not this. Not knowing what she could say to ease Mickey's pain, she wrapped Mickey in her arms and held her. Mickey held on to Treat as if her life depended on it. And perhaps it did.

After a while, Mickey's breathing became more even, and Treat thought that maybe Mickey had fallen asleep, so she didn't pull away. She wondered how anyone could survive the guilt of knowing her lover had given her life for her.

Mickey's story explained so much. Now Treat understood why Mickey wasn't able to talk about her past and had run from her, but she was very glad that this time Mickey had stayed. She was uncertain what it had cost Mickey, and them, for her to tell the story. She fervently hoped the price was not too high for either Mickey or the budding relationship between them.

When Mickey awoke, she tried to pull away, but Treat held on. She didn't want the world intruding on them.

Without thinking her question through, Treat asked, "Who was the woman I saw you with when you said you were in Montpelier?"

"I won't ask you how you know I wasn't in Montpelier because I'm pretty sure I already know. With super sleuth Denis living with you, it's hard to keep anything a secret," Mickey said. "Anyway, her name is Diana Langston. She's the US Marshal in charge of my life. She was there to pick me up to take me to DC for a meeting."

Treat was suffused with relief that it hadn't been a lover with Mickey.

"One more question and then I'll stop, okay?" Treat asked.

"Sure."

"How did you learn carpentry?"

"My grandfather was a carpenter, and he taught me. From the time I was a little girl, I was fascinated by what he could do with wood. I spent every summer with him in his wood shop. When I was in college, I took a class in sculpting and wanted to sculpt in wood. But I wanted to be a lawyer like my mom and a Marine like my dad, so I joined the Corps after law school. When I went into the Witness Protection Program, the feds asked me what I could do besides practice law, and I told them carpentry. They found the job with Sloan for me, and here I am."

"Thanks."

Treat wondered what she should call Mickey/Jo. *Would I endanger Mickey/Jo if I started calling her Jo? Who knows who might be listening either on the phone or in the grocery store?*

Treat tried to still her mind to keep all the questions she had at bay. As she was falling asleep she wondered at the miracle of having found Mickey. She continued to hold Mickey in her arms, and Mickey still clung to her.

When Treat awoke, she was on her back and knew Mickey was no longer in the bed with her. She looked around and found Mickey again standing in front of the window looking out onto the meadow. Treat quietly got out of bed and went to stand behind Mickey. She put her arms around Mickey's waist, waiting to see what Mickey would do. She silently prayed Mickey would not pull away. For a moment, Treat was sure she would, but then Mickey relaxed and leaned against her.

"Good morning. How are you doing?"

"I'm not sure. It took everything I had not to sneak out of here when I woke."

"I'm glad you stayed. Regrets?"

"About making love with you? None. About telling you my story? Some."

Treat nuzzled Mickey's neck.

"I'm glad you stayed, and I'm glad you trusted me. I could sense how hard it was for you."

Mickey twisted in Treat's arms and kissed her hard and long. Treat's body responded, and she pulled Mickey back to bed.

CHAPTER FIFTEEN

After showering, they returned the sheets to the bed, gathered discarded clothing, and got dressed. When they emerged from the bedroom, they heard Denis in the kitchen singing along with Prince on his iPod. He removed his ear buds and turned to them.

"Do you see what's outside?" Denis demanded.

"I hope you're talking about the snow and not a bear in the meadow," Treat said.

"Yes, the snow."

"Isn't it wonderful?" Mickey asked.

Denis looked at her like she'd lost her mind.

"You both look remarkably refreshed."

Treat laughed, and Mickey blushed.

"So do you, sir," Treat said. "Have a good time last night?"

"Excellent. Are you hungry?"

"Famished."

"Good, I've just made some incredible fresh blueberry pancake batter, or I'll whip you up something else. Why don't you go find the girls? They got positively depressed when you two weren't around."

"Pancakes for me, please," Treat told him.

"Me, too," Mickey chimed in.

Mickey and Treat found the dogs in the living room. The girls didn't jump up to follow them outside. "I'm thinking they've already been introduced to snow and aren't happy about it," Treat said.

"You're probably right. Let's see if they'll chase the tennis balls."

Mickey stepped outside, grabbed a tennis ball from the bucket, and threw it as far as she could. Both dogs, who had followed her out, watched the ball sail out into the meadow, but neither of them chased it. Apparently, neither was impressed with snow.

Treat and Mickey went back inside and into the library, where Denis had started a fire. Treat and Mickey stretched their feet out toward the fireplace to warm them.

Mickey took Treat's hand in hers and asked, "Treat, can you tell me about Chloe?"

Treat wasn't sure she could. She hadn't talked to anyone but Denis about Chloe. Denis had been nearly as devastated as she had been when Chloe died. They had helped each other through that dark period in their lives. She knew, though, that trust was a two-way street. She couldn't demand Mickey tell her story but then refuse to tell her own when asked. "I haven't spoken to anyone but Denis about Chloe since she died. But I want to share her with you." Mickey squeezed her hand and waited.

"Chloe and I met when we were still at the university. We were both juniors when we met. We were so young, Chloe was only eighteen and I was nineteen. I'd never met anyone like Chloe. It was as if she somehow got me. I'd been a loner most of my life because I knew I was different—different because I was smarter than most of the kids at my schools, different because I thought girls were the coolest, different because I was good enough to play sports with the guys. When I met

Chloe, she taught me I was special, and special made me different in a good way."

Treat paused. She smiled at the memories of Chloe, but she didn't want to get lost in her memories of Chloe.

"Chloe and I both thought technology was awesome. We took computer-related classes when most girls didn't even know what a computer was. We didn't even mind being called geeks or nerds. We were both good at it and knew it. During our senior year, we came up with the idea for our company, Taylor and Dandridge. The business was successful beyond our wildest dreams. But Chloe started having weird periods, and she then stopped having periods altogether. Denis and I both tried to get her to see a doctor, but she was always too busy. Then one night, she was in so much pain she had no choice, and Denis drove us to the hospital while I held Chloe in the backseat. I had never been so scared in my life."

Treat wasn't sure she wanted to—or could—continue.

Mickey leaned over and kissed her softly on the cheek. "That's okay, baby. Maybe another time."

"No. I want to tell you. It didn't take the doctors very long to reach a diagnosis. Chloe had ovarian cancer, and it had metastasized and was attacking other organs. They gave her only a few weeks to live. The hospital moved a bed into her room, and I was with her twenty-four seven. The night she died, she thanked me for loving her. She said that loving me was the best and easiest thing she'd ever done. She asked me to hold her. She died in my arms. Denis had to forcibly make me let her go. I wanted to die with her. Denis kept me alive until I could do that for myself."

Treat stopped to wipe away her tears, unable to continue.

Mickey pulled her into her arms and held her tight. "Thank you," she whispered.

"For what?" Treat asked, looking at Mickey for the first

time since she had started telling her about Chloe. Mickey had tears in her eyes.

"For telling me about Chloe."

Treat pulled back from Mickey and laid her hand on Mickey's sternum, but didn't trust her voice to speak.

"And thanks for last night," Mickey whispered.

"It was my pleasure."

"Not so much, but it will be the next time I get you alone," Mickey said with a grin.

"You underestimate your effect on me."

"I wish."

Treat heard the phone ringing in the distance but was too engrossed in Mickey to care who was calling. Denis stuck his head in the door and said, "Treat, can I speak with you a moment?"

No, not now, Denis! She wanted the intimacy with Mickey to last a little longer. But she knew Denis wouldn't have interrupted if it weren't important.

"Sorry," Treat told Mickey as she got up wondering who it had been on the phone.

"That's okay. I've been wanting to go through your library."

Chapter Sixteen

As she entered the kitchen, Treat found Denis looking pensively at the phone.

"What is it?" Treat asked.

"That was Jason from the Boston office. A while back, I asked him to find out all he could on Mickey. It took him an inordinately long time, but he just called." Denis paused.

"And?" Treat said a tad impatiently.

"I don't think you're going to like what he's found."

"We won't know if you don't tell me."

"Apparently, our friend Mickey was in the Judge Advocate's office in DC. Three years ago, she was attacked by a former Marine she'd convicted of rape and murder. She nearly died from her wounds, and the woman behind her did die. However, the attacker wasn't killed in the ensuing melee. He was sent to a high-security prison in the Midwest. Last year, he escaped, but no one knows how he did it. Speculation has been he had inside help. Mickey started getting threatening emails and texts, and the Marine Corps announced she had taken a medical leave of absence. The truth of the matter is the US Attorney General's office put her into the Witness Protection Program, and she ended up here."

"I know most of that. Mickey told me last night."

"Did you know there have been a couple of strangers in town posing as government attorneys asking around about her?"

"No."

From the doorway, Mickey said, "You're remarkably well informed, Denis. I'm pretty sure the FBI and Homeland Security wish they had your resources."

"Is it true, then?" Denis asked.

"Yes. It's all true."

"Do you know who's asking about you around town?"

"Not yet. They can't be government attorneys, though, because they'd have no reason to be asking about me. If they needed to know where I was, they'd be told."

"Are you in danger?" Treat wanted to know. "Are we all in danger?"

"Possibly. Especially if they ask the right people where I am."

"What are you going to do?"

"There's really not much I can do at this stage. I'll call Diana Langston and tell her what you've found. I guess I could move, but I don't want to start running every time someone asks after me. I don't want to leave Vermont, and I don't have any other place to go anyway."

"What I want to know is why someone has come asking for you after a year," Denis said.

"Maybe it's taken that long to find me."

"And maybe these people aren't related to the earlier incident."

"Then who could be hunting me?"

Interesting choice of words, Treat thought. *"Hunting" is a very scary-sounding word in this context.*

"Perhaps you should contact someone and ask for help," Treat said.

Mickey hesitated before answering. "They're already here. They can't find anyone who's been asking about me."

"Maybe I can find out," Denis said to no one in particular.

"Didn't you say, Denis, you were dating an attorney who was new in town?" Mickey asked.

"Yeah. He said he had only been here two months."

"Did he ask if you knew Mickey?" Treat asked.

"Not directly. We were talking about local artists, and her name came up. He didn't ask if I knew her," Denis said.

"Why would he ask you about local artists when you've only been here a little while yourself?"

"Good question. I'll try to find out who he really is," Denis said, as he turned back to finish fixing breakfast.

"Denis, could you give me a description of your attorney so I can sketch him and give it to the marshals with me?"

"I'm sure I can."

"Treat, as soon as I get Denis's description, I'll need to get back to the house and figure out what's going on," Mickey told her. "I'd like to see you again. Soon. Can you come over for dinner tonight? Denis, too."

"I'd like to see you again, too, Mickey. I can do dinner tonight. There may be another person with us, is that okay?"

Mickey raised an eyebrow but didn't ask for more information. "Of course it's okay. Come over around six?"

After breakfast, Denis asked, "Are you ready?"

"Let me get my sketchbook out of the truck," Mickey said.

When Mickey returned, she joined Denis and Treat at the dining room table. Treat watched her page through her sketchbook until she found a fresh page. Treat saw some intriguing sketches. She'd love to get her hands on the sketchbook to look at what Mickey had been working on.

"I'm ready. Concentrate on his face, please," Mickey said.

Denis and Mickey spent a half hour working on the sketch.

When they were done, Treat asked, "Is this the guy who shot you?"

"My memory of the man is pretty sketchy, but I don't think so. I'll give this to the marshals and let them find out who he is," Mickey said as she got up from the table to leave.

"Please be careful out there, Mickey."

"I will be. Denis, Treat's coming over for dinner. I'd like you to come with her."

"I'll check my calendar," he said with a grin.

At the front door, Mickey and Treat embraced. Neither wanted to let the other go.

"I'll see you at six," Treat said.

Mickey kissed Treat lightly on the lips. "I can't wait," she said. Before Treat could respond, Mickey was heading out the door with Lucy at her heels.

Denis came out of the kitchen and said, "Don't forget you're meeting the Armitage security team this afternoon at two to go over things. I hope you're still comfortable with having security."

Treat had forgotten the scheduled interview as she lay lost in Mickey's arms, but knew she had to go through with it and why. She went upstairs and lay down on her bed, and with the help of the smell of their lovemaking lingering in the air, she started to relive her time with Mickey.

The next thing she knew, Denis was gently shaking her foot to awaken her. "C'mon, Treat, it's time to get up."

"What? What time is it?"

"It's one thirty. I want to go over a few things with you before the security people get here."

"I need to take another shower to wake up," she told him. "I'll be down in a few minutes."

"All right. But don't let this be one of your forty-five-minute showers, okay?" he asked.

"Damn, you can be such a mother hen."

"Yeah, I can be, but that's what you pay me the big bucks for," he told her as he left the room.

Treat took a quick shower. As she dressed in a pair of black slacks and a red T-shirt, she noted she felt remarkably refreshed. The nap had done wonders to restore her. *Yeah, right. It was the nap that did it for you, right? How about the fact that you had the best sex of your life last night?* Treat acknowledged with a smile that the sex might have something to do with it, too.

As Treat moved down the stairs, she heard voices coming from the dining room. She headed toward the voices and paused at the door. Seated around the table were five people and Denis. The Armitage people were early.

When she entered the room, everyone stood, including Denis. She quirked an eyebrow at him, but he ignored her.

"Ladies and gentlemen, this is Treat Dandridge. Treat, these people are from the Lee Armitage Security firm. I'll let them introduce themselves."

The last person to introduce herself was Sienna O'Hara. Unlike the others, she did not give her title. That told Treat that she would be the person in charge of her detail. As the others outlined their plan for protecting her, Treat watched the woman who would keep her out of harm's way. She appeared to be around five feet six inches tall. She had chestnut-colored hair that barely brushed her shoulders. Her dark brown eyes took in everything and everyone. There was intelligence and a hint of humor in those eyes. She had an aura of controlled power, like a caged panther. Treat liked the woman. She thought she could live with having O'Hara in her space.

Treat tuned into the conversation as it was ending. Silently, Denis looked at her and raised an eyebrow. She nodded. Denis congratulated the company on winning the contract. He also told them Treat's protection would start immediately. Again, there was a round of handshakes.

"Ms. Dandridge?" O'Hara asked. "May I see you for a moment?"

"Of course," Treat told her.

"I want to make sure you're agreeable with this arrangement. You didn't say anything during the meeting, and if you're uncomfortable or disagree with the need for security, I'd like to know now."

"I'm not uncomfortable with the idea of security, Ms. O'Hara. I don't know how invasive you intend to be."

"I will try to be as non-invasive as possible. However, I will not allow your life to be put in jeopardy because your security may be inconvenient or invasive."

"I appreciate that, Ms. O'Hara."

"I will need a list of all your appointments. I will also need a list of your friends and other people you will be interacting with on a regular basis."

"I'll email those to you," Treat told her.

"I'd rather you wrote them out," O'Hara said. "Until we do a complete security check of this house, your computers, cell phones, and cars, I'd rather not give potential perpetrators any advantage."

The latter statement, more than anything else, brought home the seriousness that O'Hara brought to the business of protecting her. While her own company had insisted on the same intensity, she had never had it applied to herself before. When it became personal, it took on a whole different meaning.

"The first appointment is this evening. I will be having dinner with Mickey Heiden at her home. You need to know that she's in the Witness Protection Program."

O'Hara didn't even blink an eye when told that Mickey was in the Witness Protection Program. At the very least,

Treat thought it might surprise her that Treat knew. Treat now understood how well O'Hara was able to mask her personal feelings.

"Ms. Dandridge, I will have to contact Ms. Heiden to speak with her about her security team before we can even think of going there."

"I understand. By the way, what do I call you?" Treat asked.

"O'Hara will do," she said with a slight smile.

The two women continued talking until each was comfortable with the other. O'Hara left to walk the property. Treat found Denis in the kitchen. They sat at the counter with cups of tea.

"How are you doing with the whole security set-up?" Denis asked.

"I don't know," Treat said. "I'm just spooked enough by Mickey's story to think that having O'Hara around may not be such a bad thing."

"It gets better. The guy I went out with last night? All of the information he gave me was bogus. And before you ask, yes, I've told O'Hara what I know, and she's looking into it, too."

"You know, this is too weird, Denis. What have we gotten ourselves into here?"

"I wish I knew, girlfriend. I'm not even sure how to go about finding out."

"Don't forget, Mickey wants us at her house at six. We'll have to leave soon."

"I'm not going with you tonight."

"Why not?"

"I'm in no mood to have to watch two lesbians lusting after one another and wishing I'd disappear," Denis said with a laugh.

"Like there's going to be any lusting after anybody tonight, Den."

"What do you mean? You two haven't broken up again, have you?"

It was Treat's turn to laugh. "No, not yet. The three of us aren't going to be the only ones there."

"What do you mean? She's having a dinner party?"

"Not exactly. I'll have O'Hara and God knows who else with me. She'll probably have two marshals with her. So let's assume that there's going to be at least four security people at the party, which means there's not going to be a lot of anything going on, Den."

"Ah. You have a point. I'll go, then. Maybe one of Mickey's security team will be totally hot and interested in a little action," Denis said, waggling his eyebrows.

Treat laughed and went upstairs to get her shoes, Bella trailing along behind her. She found the shoes she wanted and sat on her bed to put them on. With a last look in the full-length mirror, she pronounced herself presentable for a dinner date. She grabbed a jacket she'd bought the week before for when it got cold. She'd had no idea it would be cold this soon. She headed back downstairs with Bella bounding down the stairs ahead of her.

"Damn," she muttered as she saw Denis waiting by the front door talking to O'Hara and another woman. "Who knew I'd ever have an entourage?"

Chapter Seventeen

Treat led her entourage out to the SUV. She opened the tailgate and helped Bella into the space while she wondered how much longer Bella would need assistance jumping into the car. She started around the car to the driver's side.

"Treat, please ride in the backseat. Denis, you get to drive," O'Hara said.

"Why?" she and Denis asked in unison.

"If someone comes after you, Treat, I want you to get down on the floorboard and out of sight so I don't have to worry about you while I fend off the bad guys," O'Hara said.

"Oh, okay," Treat said and tossed Denis the keys over the hood. She raised one eyebrow at him as if to say, "See what you've wrought?"

Denis grinned at her, and Treat realized that he was really enjoying the cloak-and-dagger aspect of all this. She didn't have the heart to tell him she knew the "bad guys" almost always killed the driver first.

Before O'Hara got into the car, she leaned in and said, "Denis, you need to wear a seat belt."

"What?" he said, incredulity lacing his voice. Treat knew he'd been ignoring the seat belt laws because he refused to put a seat belt on and wrinkle his shirt.

When it became obvious O'Hara would not get into the car before he put his seat belt on, he snapped it into place. "Oh, all right. Damned bossy women in my life," he muttered under his breath.

Treat grinned. Score one for O'Hara. Not many people won a battle of wills with Denis.

As they drove off the property, O'Hara said, "Ms. Dandridge, perhaps you should consider hiring a professional driver."

"Uh, Treat, that's probably a good idea," Denis said.

Treat refrained from making chicken sounds. She thought Denis was probably already too freaked out to take kindly to being ribbed about it.

So, instead of chicken sounds, Treat said, "O'Hara, do you know a driver who is available and would come live in the wilds of Vermont?"

"As a matter of fact, I do," O'Hara told her. "One of the best in the business has become available over the last couple of days. I'll give her a call, if you like, and see if we can snag her before someone else hires her."

"Dare I ask why she's available?" Denis asked.

"Her employer died," O'Hara said. Twelve beats later, she added, "In his sleep of heart failure. He was ninety-eight."

She heard Denis harrumph at O'Hara's unspoken "gotcha!"

Treat saw that O'Hara was concentrating on the side-view mirror on her side of the car. Treat glanced over her shoulder and saw a white sedan behind them. In a more urban setting, she wouldn't have even noted the car. But since her house was the last one on a country road, there shouldn't have been any cars behind Treat's SUV. Perhaps it was a lost tourist, she told herself hopefully, but not believing it for a moment.

"Denis, slow down to about fifteen miles per hour," O'Hara said, "but don't brake to do so."

"What…?" Denis began.

Treat saw his eyes widen as he glanced into his rearview mirror and saw the white car.

Denis slowed down as he was told.

"Okay, now speed up by ten miles and do it slowly," O'Hara said to him.

Treat saw O'Hara writing in a small notebook.

"Good. Maintain this speed to the main road. Which way would you normally turn to go to Ms. Heiden's house?"

"Left," Treat said.

"Okay. When we get to the main road, turn right and don't forget to put your turn signal on," O'Hara said.

"Roger," Denis said with a grin in the rearview mirror at Treat.

Two hundred feet before they reached the main road, Denis flipped on the turn signal indicating that he was going to turn right. Denis executed the right-hand turn. The car behind them also turned right.

"Slow down slightly when you see the first driveway, Denis," O'Hara told him. "I want you to pull into the driveway. As soon as the other car is past, back out, reverse direction, and hit the accelerator."

"Yes, ma'am," Denis said and did exactly as he was told.

"Well, done, Denis," O'Hara said. She retrieved her cell phone and hit a speed-dial number. She spoke quietly into the phone.

Denis did the same. "Bruce," he said, "it's Denis. Listen, I need info on a Vermont license plate." He rattled off the number, listened for a moment, and then said, "Thanks, buddy."

Treat was impressed that Denis had had the presence of mind to make a mental note of the white car's license plate. When Denis and O'Hara got off their respective phones, O'Hara showed him what she'd written in her notebook. Denis nodded. He'd gotten the same information from Bruce. They didn't share their information with Treat. She was sure they'd tell her when the details were confirmed—or at least she hoped they would share.

Treat saw a piece of wood sticking out from beneath the driver's seat. It was Mickey's directions to her house that she'd given Treat when they had first met. She picked it up and used it to direct Denis to Mickey's house. Now was not the time to be wandering lost in the countryside outside Brattleboro.

Chapter Eighteen

When they arrived at Mickey's, she was waiting for them on her deck. Treat exited the vehicle on the right side and went to the rear of the car to let Bella out. Bella bounded around the car to Mickey, wriggling her entire body in greeting her second most favorite person in the whole wide world. Mickey bent down on one knee and rubbed Bella's ears in greeting.

"Lucy's up at the house," Mickey told Bella. As if cued, Lucy came running out onto the deck and barked once. Bella looked at Treat for permission.

"Okay," Treat told the young dog. Bella took off at top speed to get to her buddy.

"You're late," Mickey whispered to Treat as they hugged.

"A bit of an incident on the road," Treat told her.

"Come up to the house and tell me about it," Mickey told her. "Who's your friend? Are they coming in?" she asked, pointing with her chin toward the car where Denis and O'Hara sat with their cell phones glued to their ears.

"Yeah, they'll be in. I think they've developed some kind of convivial rivalry. They both put someone onto finding out who owns the car that followed us. The woman's name is

O'Hara, and she's head of my new security team. C'mon, let's not wait for them."

"You hired a security team because of what I told you last night?" Mickey asked.

"No, this has been in the works for a couple of weeks," Treat insisted.

"Why?"

"Uh, I was featured in a recent *Forbes* magazine article, which prompted Denis to insist on security." Treat wasn't entirely sure why she'd been vague about the subject of the *Forbes* article. She didn't want Mickey to treat her differently, especially not after the night before.

The two women headed up the path to Mickey's house. By the time they reached the deck, O'Hara and Denis were both out of the car and walking toward them, apparently comparing notes.

When they reached Treat and Mickey, Treat introduced O'Hara to Mickey.

"I've got news that O'Hara ought to hear," Mickey said.

"What is it?" Treat asked.

"Blackhorn was sighted in the area by a young Brattleboro cop who is in the habit of studying the FBI's most wanted posters," Mickey said. "The local police informed the nearest US Marshal's office. They sent two additional marshals from Montpelier. Then a couple of FBI agents showed up and sent the marshals on their way. So I've got additional guests."

"Damn," Denis said.

"Double damn," O'Hara muttered. "The description you provided on the attorney you saw last night confirms Blackhorn is in the area."

"I had dinner with Blackhorn the other night?" Denis asked. "I had dinner and sex with a rapist and killer? Oh. My. God."

"Steady, Denis," Treat told him, sure that he was about to hyperventilate.

"Actually, no, you didn't. Sorry to disappoint you," O'Hara said. "The guy you had dinner with is a private investigator. He confirmed that he'd been hired by Blackhorn without knowing who he was."

"Oh," Denis said, sounding a little sheepish after his outburst.

"Come on in, I need to finish making dinner," Mickey said.

Before they could move inside, a dark SUV with tinted windows drove slowly past, and everyone tensed. The car passed by and out of sight.

O'Hara went to talk to the agent at the end of the deck. The four-legged girls took off around the corner of the house for no reason other than their noses thought they smelled something interesting. The agent at the edge of the woods kept her eyes on the road.

"Denis, why don't you chill out in a rocking chair out here and keep an eye on the girls. Don't let them head down to the gate and the road," Mickey told him.

Denis sank gratefully into the rocker, leaning back and closing his eyes. He opened his eyes but continued rocking gently.

"Come help me put the salad together," Mickey told Treat, adding, "please."

As the two women turned to go into the house, shots rang out. O'Hara and the agent she had been talking to headed for Treat and Mickey at a run, yelling "Get down!"

Treat and Mickey both dropped to the deck. Denis, too, all but fell out of his chair. Treat saw the agent at the edge of the woods pull his weapon out and take off at a run for the source of the gunfire. He was followed by the agent on the deck who rushed down the steps, two at a time, with her weapon drawn, too.

"Stay down until I tell you it's safe to get up," O'Hara commanded them. Her gun, too, was drawn and held at the ready.

Treat had no intention of getting to her feet any time soon. Bella and Lucy came pounding around the corner of the house curious as to what was going on and the new tone of the voices they'd heard. When they saw their owners flat on the deck, they assumed it was play time. Both women grabbed their respective puppies, each moving to cover her puppy with her body in a primordial response to protect the babies in their midst.

After a few minutes, O'Hara told them, "Let's move inside. Stay away from any windows," she said, looking at the house for the first time, adding, "if possible."

"What a fucking nightmare this house is. Who would put a protectee in this place?" Treat heard O'Hara murmur as she came up behind her.

Treat remembered there was no space in the house that did not have huge windows in it—including the bathroom. She looked around and realized they were exposed to anybody in the woods with a rifle.

"Everyone okay?" asked the agent who had earlier been talking to O'Hara as she came into the house. Both the agent and O'Hara returned their weapons to their holsters.

Everyone in the house assured her they were alive.

"We're assuming the shooter drove off in the black Escalade that cruised by before the shooting. We could only get a partial plate number, though." The agent filled O'Hara in on what had happened outside. "It may take us a day or two to get the details on that Escalade," the agent finished.

Denis and O'Hara glanced at each other and smiled.

Apparently, a bond had been struck over the tracking down of the white car.

"By the way, my name is Jones," the agent told Treat. "Honest," she added as Treat looked at her skeptically. "I assume you're Treat Dandridge."

"I've got a suggestion," Treat said impulsively. "Why don't we move this party to my house?"

"Why?" Mickey demanded.

"Because, sweetie, I feel more than a little exposed standing here in front of floor-to-ceiling windows with a shooter out there somewhere. Besides, it'll be dark soon, and we'd be even more exposed once we turn on the lights."

"Oh. That," Mickey said. "I think we could easily move dinner to your house. That's assuming, of course, that you have a barbecue," she added with a smile.

Treat was shaking her head even as Denis was saying, "As a matter of fact, I bought a Weber yesterday."

"Really?" Treat asked, surprised she hadn't seen it on the patio when she'd gone outside with Bella earlier, although considering the amount of snow on the ground, she understood why he hadn't set it up.

"Yep. It's in the garage waiting to be put together. I'm pretty sure you and Mickey can handle that while I make the salad and add baked potatoes to the menu."

"Do you have a problem with us moving to my house?" Treat asked O'Hara.

"No, I don't," O'Hara told her. She turned to Jones and asked, "Do you?"

"Absolutely not. Let's do it now," Jones replied.

It didn't take them long to pack up the dinner Mickey had planned to serve them, get the dogs into the car, and head back to Treat's home. The backseat was a little crowded with the two dogs, Treat, and Mickey, but the dogs settled down between the two women for a nap. They arrived at Treat's house without incident.

Denis, Mickey, and Treat took their uncooked dinner into the kitchen. Denis put away the things needing refrigeration and took other things out of the fridge and put them on the center island. He also set out six rather large potatoes. Treat raised a questioning eyebrow at the number of potatoes he had laid out.

"They've got to eat, too." He nodded toward Stevens, the second FBI agent, and O'Hara, who were quietly talking together on the patio.

Even as Treat and Mickey watched them, Stevens moved off into the woods at a trot.

O'Hara sensed she was being watched and turned toward them. She came into the kitchen and said, "May I have a word alone with you, Treat?"

"Of course," Treat told her with an apologetic look at Mickey.

"That's okay," Mickey told her. "It looks like Denis could use a hand. I'll stay here and help fix dinner."

Treat led O'Hara into the study. O'Hara closed the door behind them.

"There are a couple of anomalies that are making me nervous about Mickey's team. Protection is always provided to people in the Witness Protection Program by the US Marshal's office, and they've been called off. Then there are certain protocols that agents are trained to follow, and they're not doing that. Jones has left the house for unknown reasons, leaving only Stevens to protect Mickey. The problem is that I don't know what's going on, and I don't know how to find out without going through a bunch of red tape. That being said, however, I intend to find out, and fast, before it can put all our lives in jeopardy. Before you say anything, I've called for backup from my firm, and they're on their way."

"I don't know you well yet," Treat said, "so I'll just say this. It sounds to me like you've got something else on your mind. Will you tell me what it is?"

"You're very perceptive. At this time, however, I'm unwilling to put my concerns into words. Let's just say I'm sticking to you and Denis like glue, so be prepared."

Treat didn't know how to respond, so she nodded to let O'Hara know that she'd heard her.

When Treat returned to the kitchen, Mickey was cutting up tomatoes while Denis was shaving carrots into a large salad bowl.

"What's going on?" Mickey asked.

"I'm not sure," Treat told her, unsure why she wasn't telling Mickey the truth. Was it because O'Hara had asked her not to, or was it because she didn't completely trust Mickey yet? "But we're supposed to stay inside until Jones returns," Treat added.

Denis, who knew Treat too well, simply raised an eyebrow to let her know that he knew she was being evasive and then returned to shaving carrots.

Jones came through the door leading in from the patio. "The road is clear. I think we can rest easy for a little while," she said. "Where's Stevens?"

"Right here," Stevens said, coming into the kitchen from the front of the house.

"See anything around the perimeter?"

"Nope. All clear."

Denis turned from the stove and said, "If it's okay with you three, can these two go out to the garage to put the Weber together?"

"Yeah, that'd be fine," Jones told him.

"Thank God," Treat and Denis said in unison and burst out laughing.

"Come on, Mickey, let's get the Weber in working order," Treat told her.

Once they had it assembled, they set the grill in front of the French doors leading into the living room. Because of the cold and snow, Mickey didn't want to be out in the yard cooking. Mickey shook briquettes into the grill, poured lighter fluid over the pile, and set it on fire.

Treat and Mickey sat down in the rockers in the living room, talking quietly.

As dusk morphed into night, Denis asked Mickey if the coals were ready. Mickey went outside to check on the coals and drop the grill in place. She fetched the steaks and chicken from the kitchen and put them on the grill. When she entered the house, she said, "Damn, it's cold out there!" and shook snow off her head and shoulders.

Both Denis and Treat were uncharacteristically quiet throughout dinner. Finally, though, Treat said, "Den, did you ever think in a million years that your life would be in danger?"

"Every time I got out on the 405 freeway in a rain storm."

"That's true. Californians do not know how to drive in inclement weather. They're spoiled. I would venture to guess there are more accidents in the first rain storm of the year than any other time of year," Treat told Mickey.

"We have the same problem here with the tourists. They love to come here to ski, but, Lordy, the folks from non-snow states can't drive in the stuff, and they don't have the sense to be cautious when they do."

They continued keeping the conversation light while they

finished eating. When they took their dishes into the kitchen, there were kudos all around for Denis's dinner.

After dinner, Mickey agreed to stay the night when Treat asked. They retreated to the living room. Both were quiet. Treat's mind turned to what was going on. *It is clear this Blackhorn is obsessed with killing Mickey. And now he knows where she is. Can Mickey be protected from a madman intent on murdering her? How long before he makes a move?*

CHAPTER NINETEEN

The next morning, after seeing Mickey, Lucy, and their guardians off to their own house, Treat fixed herself a cup of tea while Denis sat with his first mug of coffee. Bored with watching Denis putter around his kitchen, Treat went to her study.

At ten, O'Hara knocked on the door. "Treat, do you have time to talk to the driver I mentioned? She took the liberty of driving up here on the off chance you'd be able to see her."

"Of course, bring her in. I'd like for you to be here while I talk to her."

"Right," O'Hara said as she turned to leave the room.

O'Hara was back within a minute with a woman of average height and weight. She had short black hair and startling green eyes, and was dressed in a pair of neat black slacks, a white shirt, and a black jacket. She had an aura of being a no-nonsense person who knew what she was doing.

Treat spent thirty minutes with her and hired her on the spot. Her name was Tamryn Mueller, but she asked to be called Tam.

Later that afternoon, O'Hara came into the kitchen where she found Treat, Denis, and Tam talking over cups of tea. O'Hara was followed by a man unknown to Treat. He approached Treat and held out his hand.

"Ms. Dandridge, my name is Daniel Chastain. I'm the supervisor of the team assigned to protect you. I'd like to talk to you about yesterday's incidents."

"Certainly," Treat told him.

"Shall we go into a more private room?" Chastain asked, looking pointedly at the other people at the table.

"No. Let's do it here," Treat told the man. She didn't like Chastain. She knew she'd only just met him, but nevertheless, she didn't like him. She usually bristled when someone came at her with an attitude, and Daniel Chastain certainly had plenty of that.

"We don't usually discuss these matters in front of the, ah, help," Chastain told her, looking again at Denis, Tam, and O'Hara.

Treat saw O'Hara grimace. She glanced at Denis and saw him grinning—he always enjoyed watching Treat put an asshole in his place.

"Mr. Chastain, while you may be the supervisor of the security team, need I remind you that I hired you, your team, and your firm. Add to that this is my home, and that means I call the shots when my life is not in immediate danger, as it is not now. Understand?" Treat said, her voice icy.

"Yes, ma'am," Chastain told her, his voice equally icy. "But I don't think it is appropriate to discuss business in front of your household help."

"Who I choose to discuss my business with is not up to you, Mr. Chastain. Do you have your cell phone with you?" Treat asked.

Chastain was clearly nonplussed by the change in her tone and the change of subject. "Of course I do, Ms. Dandridge," he said as he pulled his phone from his pocket to prove it.

"Please dial Mr. Lee's number," Treat told him. She was asking him to call the owner of Armitage, the firm Chastain and O'Hara worked for.

"What for?" Chastain demanded without losing the annoying tone of voice that reminded Treat of a snake oil or used car salesman.

Denis came around the kitchen island with his phone in his hand. He pressed a speed-dial number and handed the phone to Treat.

"Mr. Lee?" Treat asked. "This is Treat Dandridge. I'm fine." She paused to listen to the man on the other end of the call.

"What you can do for me, Mr. Lee, is to remove Daniel Chastain from my security team."

Treat again paused to listen to Mr. Lee's response to her request.

"Let me put this another way, Mr. Lee. You and your security firm are fired, effective right now. Please call Mr. Chastain and order him off my property."

Treat snapped the cell phone shut and handed it back to Denis, who grinned.

After Chastain and the man who had accompanied him into the kitchen had left the room, she told Denis, "Den, see that those men leave the house."

Treat turned to O'Hara and said, "O'Hara, have you ever thought about having your own security firm?"

"Of course I have. But I don't have the capital to open my own firm," O'Hara said.

"You do now. We'll work out the details over the next week or so."

"I can't," O'Hara said.

"You can, O'Hara. Don't walk away from the gift horse who is willing to make your dream come true. This opportunity may never come your way again. I'll be in my study. Come see me when you decide what you want to do."

Treat turned and walked out of the kitchen. She heard Tam tell O'Hara not to be an ass and to accept Treat's offer. Treat went to her study and sat in the chair behind the desk.

"Well, that was fun," Denis said as he entered the study with a mug of steaming tea in his hand. "What was it all about?"

"Den, you know how much it pisses me off when men talk down to me. When Chastain told me that I shouldn't talk about our security matters in front of the 'help,' there was no turning back."

"Well, Treat, I am the 'help,' when you get right down to it. As are O'Hara and Tam," Denis said.

"No, Denis, you are so much more than that to me. By the way, have you seen Bella lately?"

"She's decided that her new preference for her sleeping pleasure is the living room couch. There's a patch of sun she's claimed as her own. By the way, can I get in on the deal you're putting together with O'Hara?"

"If she'll have you, I don't see why not."

"Treat?" O'Hara said from the doorway.

"Come on in, O'Hara."

"I've had the opportunity to talk to a few people, and I'd like to take you up on your offer. I'd like to have my own firm," O'Hara told her with a grin. "Or at least co-own it for now."

"Great," Treat said. "Denis will have my attorney draw up an agreement, and once your attorney has approved it, you'll be in business. I'm very glad you decided to accept the offer," Treat told her as she reached out to shake her new business partner's hand. "By the way, Denis would like to be an investor in your endeavor, too. Do you have a problem with that?"

"Not at all. Besides, I could use his expertise."

"Great!" Denis uncharacteristically gushed.

Treat was surprised Denis wanted to be a partner in O'Hara's firm. For years, he had steadfastly refused to be anything other than Treat's housekeeper.

O'Hara told them, "Some of the phone calls I made were to what will be your new security team. I told them that we'd meet here at two o'clock this afternoon. With your permission, of course."

"That was fast work," Treat said.

"There are a lot of unhappy people at Lee's firm."

"I'll go give Miriam a call," Denis said.

"Denis, don't you want to sit in on the planning meetings?" Treat asked.

"Not really. You two go ahead. Fill me in later. I need to cook!" Denis said with a grin. "By the way, O'Hara, congratulations," he said before leaving the room.

"Thanks, Denis."

"O'Hara, do we need to discuss anything before the team gets here?" Treat wanted to know.

"I've taken the liberty of making a list," O'Hara told her as she pulled her notebook out of her pocket and flipped it open.

"Let's get to it, then," Treat said, settling back in her chair.

"Before we do that, I'd like to offer Stevens a job as my second-in-command. I don't know whether she'll want to leave the FBI, but I like the way she handles herself. Do you have a problem with that?"

"You're in charge of personnel. Hire whoever you want working with you," Treat told her. "Now, let's get down to the details. Tell me what your thoughts are."

CHAPTER TWENTY

Treat had decided not to attend O'Hara's meeting with her potential employees. She remained in her study going over documents faxed by her attorney.

An hour later, Denis interrupted her and said he needed to speak with her and O'Hara.

"I was just out front getting something from the car when I caught a glimpse of a black SUV cruising by the head of the driveway. I didn't get a good look, but I'm sure it's black and a SUV."

O'Hara called two of the people out of the dining room, briefly told them what they were looking for, and sent them out to see if they could find the black SUV. She pulled her cell phone out of her pocket and pressed a speed-dial number.

"Jones, O'Hara here. We've just had a black SUV cruise by the property. I've got a couple of people scrambled trying to find out where it's gone. If the driver didn't see Mickey's car here, he will be headed your way."

O'Hara listened to Jones for a minute and then snapped her phone closed.

"They are in town with Mickey. They've just finished doing the grocery shopping. They should be on their way here within ten minutes."

O'Hara returned to the dining room to brief the rest of the people on the two incidents of the previous day. Treat went in search of Denis, who had left them after he told them what he had seen. He was, as usual, in the kitchen. When she came through the door, he automatically turned the heat on beneath the teakettle. Tam, the driver, was seated on one of the stools.

"Can I ask if any of what's going on in that meeting will affect me?" Tam asked.

"No. You're on my personal payroll."

"Thanks," Tam said.

Treat put a hip on one of the stools at the center island to wait for her tea. Bella strolled in and stretched, reaching out behind her with first one long brown leg and then the other. She gave a mighty yawn and moseyed over to her food dish. When she found it empty, Bella gave Denis a reproachful look and lay down on the bed Denis had put in the corner for her. She cast him a baleful look and heaved a sigh. She was the perfect picture of a woman wronged. Treat laughed out loud.

"Mickey's on her way over and is bringing the groceries you asked for. O'Hara's got two people out looking for the black SUV. Have you had any luck with narrowing the possibilities of who owns the SUV from the partial license plate number we got yesterday?" Treat said.

"If you don't mind, I think I'll go catch up on my email," Tam said.

"Of course not," Treat told the driver, and watched as Bella followed Tam out of the kitchen. When Tam didn't go outside, Bella came back in hopes Denis would drop some tasty morsel on the floor.

"The search we were running finished about ten minutes ago. Interestingly, there are no black SUVs registered in Vermont with numbers in the order Jones gave us. That's why

O'Hara thought maybe it's an out-of-Vermont car. I hope the two people O'Hara sent out have better vision."

"We need to decide where all these people will be sleeping," Treat said.

"First, O'Hara needs to tell us whether the people off shift will be returning to their homes or whether she'll want them here around the clock until the guy who's after Mickey is caught," Denis said.

"I've told O'Hara they can use the other house as her offices until she finds something suitable in town. That means, I'm sorry to say, we'll need to go to Boston to do some more shopping."

"Oh, no!" Denis exclaimed in mock horror. "Not another shopping spree."

"Very funny, Denis. Do you mind?" Treat asked.

"Of course not. Actually, I already made a list of the bare essentials needed for the house. I think I can order most of the stuff over the phone from the places we visited when furnishing this place."

"Great!" Treat exclaimed, relieved she didn't have to go to Boston to shop.

"Until the furniture is delivered, I'll move upstairs, and the others will be in the bedrooms down here," Denis said, obviously having already thought about the logistics of having eight extra people on hand.

"Denis, were you your usual efficient self when O'Hara was assigned to me and found out what you could about her?"

Treat had realized earlier she knew little or nothing about O'Hara other than what she'd seen during the previous two days.

"Of course. I wasn't about to turn our safety over to some unknown entity."

"Well? What do we know about her?" Treat asked.

"We don't know anything about her. I, however, know quite a bit," Denis told her with a smile.

"Oh, come on. Stop teasing," Treat said.

Denis laughed at her. "You really have zero patience, you know?"

"If you don't tell me, I'll turn off your refrigerator," she threatened.

"Oh no, not that," Denis told her, throwing each hand up to his face in mock horror.

Treat gave him a look he knew intimidated a lot of people, but he'd seen it so many times over the last six years it now failed in its mission.

"She comes from a family of high achievers. She's the only one I can find who isn't a doctor or a lawyer, which would pretty much make her a black sheep. She's Yale educated. She's been with the Armitage firm for nearly five years, she is licensed by the states of Vermont, New York, and Massachusetts. She has a permit to carry a gun issued in each of those states and several others as well. She also has a federal gun permit. She has completed a number of security-related courses given by the FBI, which, I might add, she took on her own time and paid for herself."

"Sounds like a go-getter to me," Treat said.

"I'm glad we're helping her out. I like her," Denis said.

"Me, too," Treat replied. "Now tell me what you found on Tam."

"How do you know...?" Denis began, but stopped when he saw Treat eyeing his refrigerator. "She has a doctorate in archaeology from the University of California in Irvine. She was trained as a defensive driver by a well-known, highly respected driving school in Massachusetts, has gun permits in several states and a federal permit as well. She's volunteered to sleep on the couch until the small house is ready for O'Hara's people and then she'll move out there with them," Denis finished.

"Sorry to barge in," O'Hara said from the kitchen door. "But the two operatives have returned. They've got a good license plate number for us," she said, as she handed a slip of paper to Denis. "And none of the numbers match what we were given yesterday."

"I'll have it run right away. I can't wait to see who this creep is," Denis told her as he took the piece of paper from her. "Listen, would you mind if I talked to your techno person? We need to get you set up with computers and servers and the like sooner rather than later."

"Of course not, Denis. I know she's been fretting about not having any technology," O'Hara told him with a smile.

"I'm sure that's an understatement. Maybe she and I should go shopping to get the basics."

"She'd be in seventh heaven, but you'll need to take an operative with you. Would you mind taking my office manager with you, too? He'll need to get some stuff as well."

"The more the merrier. I'll go talk to them about their needs and get them to start making lists," Denis told her on his way out of the room.

"You've certainly made his day," Treat said.

"We've actually made Jade and Mack's day as well. Do you think Denis would mind taking my surveillance guy with him also? There's a place in Boston he swears by."

"Denis will be positively orgasmic at getting to go to a secret-agent store, trust me."

"Great. Listen, can we talk?"

"Of course. In the study?" Treat asked.

"No, here is fine. Where's Tam, by the way?"

"She's in the living room checking her email, et cetera."

"I know Mickey and her team are on their way. I wanted you to know Jones gave us a wrong license plate number yesterday. The number Stevens gave her was right although incomplete. I'm not sure what it means—maybe Jones is only being a fed who hates cooperating with anyone who isn't a fed. It could also mean she's dirty and working with whoever is in the Escalade. Can you tell me what you know of Mickey? Why is someone after her?"

Treat told O'Hara everything she knew about Mickey's situation.

"Here's what I know," O'Hara said. "Sheridan Blackhorn is their one and only suspect. He escaped from prison nearly a year ago and they haven't been able to recapture him. They suspect, though, he had inside help in breaking out. They haven't found out who Blackhorn's accomplice is yet either. And, it turns out, the attorney Denis had dinner with isn't an attorney at all, but a private investigator hired by Blackhorn to find Mickey. Since he's a former Marine, he's probably armed to the teeth and has evaded the feds for a year and is now in our neighborhood," O'Hara said.

Treat could practically hear the wheels turning in O'Hara's head as she assessed the situation. Before she could tell Treat her thinking, they heard the sound of a horn sounding in the driveway. They headed for the front door. A couple of people joined them from the dining room. One of them got to the front door first and peered through the peephole there.

"It's a blue truck," he told those behind them.

"Mickey drives a blue truck," Treat said.

The man at the door opened it, and Lucy came charging into the house, sliding to a halt when she realized how many people were in front of her she didn't know.

"It's okay, Lucy," Treat told the startled dog.

"I'll let the girls outside," Denis said, leaving the dining room.

Mickey strode into the house with her arms full of brown paper bags from Hannaford's, the local grocery store. She stopped long enough to kiss Treat lightly on the lips and continued through the foyer and into the kitchen.

When Mickey returned, she said to the assembled group, "There are more groceries in the car."

No one moved. Perhaps they didn't want to go out into the cold. Maybe they were taken with Mickey's beauty.

"Denis, your groceries have arrived. I could use some help getting them into the kitchen, and it seems your statuary here are loath to help unload the truck," she said as she continued out the front door.

The entire room burst into motion with people vying to get out to the car to help bring in the groceries. Treat decided the best thing she could do was to get out of everyone's way, so she took a seat on one of the steps leading to the upper floor. O'Hara came and leaned against the wall not far from her.

The carriers returned, each carrying at least two bags of groceries.

"It looks like Denis is planning for a siege," O'Hara commented.

"Nah," Treat told her. "He likes to cook, so having people in the house is the perfect excuse to cook a lot. A lot of cooking requires a lot of food."

"You know you don't have to feed us, too," O'Hara told her.

"I figure after you get set up in the little house, we won't be feeding your crew much, so why not let Denis have a little fun now?"

CHAPTER TWENTY-ONE

Denis had managed to convince several of the people bringing in the groceries to work as his sous chefs. When Treat stuck her head in the door, there was much chattering going on, many knives slicing and dicing, and a half dozen happy people.

Treat was startled when she looked out her living room windows and saw strangers in her yard and at the tree line. She remembered who they were and relaxed. Mickey found her staring out the French doors across the snow-covered expanse of her yard. She walked up behind Treat, pressed herself against Treat's back, and put her arms around her. They stood like that for several minutes, savoring the peacefulness of the moment.

It wasn't long before someone interrupted their moment by clearing her throat behind them. They moved apart to find Jones standing in the doorway.

"I've been recalled to DC," she told them. "Two replacements are on the way. I'll be back by Sunday. O'Hara will be in charge while I'm away. Stay safe."

Jones was gone before either woman could respond.

"What the hell? Where is she going? And more importantly, why is she going?" Mickey asked.

"What's going on? Isn't she supposed to stay with you until her replacement arrives?"

"I don't like this," Mickey said. "I need to talk with O'Hara."

Before Mickey could move, O'Hara came through the doors. "Jones told me she was leaving. I've obtained some information from a former colleague who says unequivocally Stevens is clean."

O'Hara paused to let it sink in that Jones was the dirty agent.

"I think we should prepare for some action tonight. I'd like everyone to gather in the dining room," she said.

Once everyone had crowded into the dining room, O'Hara briefed them on Jones's sudden departure and the likelihood she was dirty.

"While my colleague's take on Stevens doesn't clear her, it does make Jones the more likely candidate to be on the take. I think it's unlikely we'd be dealing with two dirty feds at once."

"O'Hara, I'm at a disadvantage because I don't know the names of the people sitting here. Can you help me out?" Treat asked.

O'Hara blushed deeply but introduced everyone at the table. She told them, "The two people outside are Josephine and Larry."

"If you don't need me, can I return to my boiling pots?" Denis asked.

"Of course you can. Treat, you and Mickey don't have to stay either. I'll brief you when we've decided what we're doing," O'Hara said.

Mickey and Treat got up from the table and followed Denis out of the room and into the kitchen.

"Denis, do you need help now that your sous chefs have been pre-empted?"

"No, Tam and I are handling things in here. We could use the company, though," he said.

"I'm not sure whether to believe him about not needing help or be insulted. What are you fixing?" Mickey asked.

"The big pot has a cheesy potato soup in it, the pot on the back burner is chili, and I'm fixing us *scaloppini de pollo*."

"Yum," Mickey said.

"Are you two okay?" Denis wanted to know.

Treat and Mickey looked at each other questioningly. They hadn't talked about how they were doing. Neither wanted to be the first to voice her feelings about what was happening around them.

They were saved from having to answer by Lucy and Bella trotting into the kitchen to see what was going on there. The second they crossed the threshold, their noses began twitching as they took in all the wonderful aromas.

Treat and Mickey retreated to the living room before Denis could change his mind and put them to work chopping, dicing, or shredding.

"You didn't answer Denis's question," Treat said as she joined Mickey at the French doors.

"Nor did you."

"No, nor did I. So, how are you?"

"I am scared shitless," Mickey said in a low voice. "We're in one of the most beautiful places in the country, and I'm scanning the woods looking for a man with a rifle who has already tried to kill me once and very nearly succeeded. I've got a federal agent who is supposed to be guarding me from that maniac but who has bailed on me and may be working with or for him. I guess I'm not doing so well."

"No surprise there. Thank God we have O'Hara with us," Treat said as she took Mickey's hand.

"I'll be glad when this is all over and we can concentrate on other things," Mickey said.

"What other things would you like to concentrate on?"

"Your body, for one. Us, for another," Mickey replied.

"Anything in particular?"

"Several things leap to mind, actually. Like, where is this going?" Mickey asked, waving her hand vaguely in the air.

"Does 'this' mean our relationship?"

"Yeah. I think I need to know if all we're doing is dating for a while before you move on, or is it possible this may be something for the long term," Mickey said with a slight tremor in her voice.

"Damn, girl, you've been doing some heavy thinking while you've been away. I thought you were the one who didn't want to commit to having a relationship—long or short," Treat said.

"I was wrong. I do want to be in a relationship, but only with you," Mickey said and paused. "And only if it will last."

Treat wasn't sure what to think of Mickey's sudden change of mind. On the one hand, she was happy about it because it was what she wanted. On the other hand, she wasn't sure she should trust the sudden about-face Mickey had taken.

"I note you haven't answered Denis's question yet," Mickey said.

"I'm frightened about having Blackhorn in the neighborhood, but not, I'm sure, at the level you are. I haven't been required to live with the thought of him as long as you have."

Treat held up her hand when Mickey opened her mouth to speak. "As for us," she said, turning her body so she could see Mickey's face, "I'd like to think we've got something special here. So let's get the hell out of Dodge."

"I don't want to start running, Treat. I know my life is in danger, and so is yours and everyone else's, for that matter. I can't help thinking Blackhorn will continue to hunt me until one of us is dead. I'd prefer that, in the end, it be him on the cold slab rather than me," Mickey said.

"So would I, baby, so would I."

"Dinner's ready. O'Hara wants an all-hands meeting afterward," Denis said and turned toward the kitchen.

"Can we talk about us later?" Mickey asked.

"We'd better," Treat said.

The two women went to find the dogs and found them behind the couch in the living room where they had rushed when all the shouting had started. Once they were held and reassured, Treat and Mickey went to the kitchen with the puppies dashing in before them.

"Aren't we eating rather early?" Treat asked Denis. She looked at the clock and saw it was only 5:45.

"We are, but there's a reason. O'Hara wants everything and everyone in place before it gets dark. To do that, we need to be fed before it gets dark. So here we are, eating like most people do—with the six o'clock news."

While Mickey and Treat stood watching, there was a steady stream of people coming into the kitchen to get bowls of chili or potato soup, and Denis's freshly baked French bread or cornbread. Denis, Mickey, and Treat ate at the kitchen counter while the others ate in Treat's dining room, also known as OHS headquarters. There was another steady stream of people coming back into the kitchen for seconds, and in three cases, thirds.

Forty-five minutes later, everyone was ensconced in a chair in the dining room except the two OHS personnel who had replaced Josephine and Larry outside so they could have dinner. O'Hara ran a tight meeting, no distractions, no going off on unrelated tangents. She held everyone on point, and the meeting was quickly over.

"O'Hara," Denis asked, "Why don't we just make a run for it?"

"I've discussed this with Mickey and her agents. Individually, they believe staying here is the best course of action here. We can protect you better in this setting than if we took off for, say, Boston. We'd be exposed in the cars even with Tam driving you."

Denis nodded he understood.

Once O'Hara was sure everyone knew their assignments, the meeting broke up. A couple of people asked Denis if there were any leftovers, and when they got a positive response, they headed for the kitchen. Mickey, Treat, Denis, and O'Hara took themselves off to Treat's study to talk.

"I've spoken with the Brattleboro police chief and the Vermont State Police. The Bratt police chief initially wanted to send his people here to help out. Once he found out the feds were involved, he backed off a little but will have his people on standby. I agreed to call him when—and if—the feds weren't able to handle the situation here. The VSP were no easier to convince, but the feds' presence made them back off, too. They'll stand by with reinforcements and a helicopter to come in if the task is beyond the feds' capabilities. The real bottom line here is because the feds are involved, the locals have to stay away."

"What do you think is going to happen tonight?" Denis asked.

"I think nothing is going to happen tonight. I think Blackhorn will probably wait until the wee hours of the morning before making a move to be assured everyone in the house is asleep. However, he may be cagier than I thought and figure out it would be our thinking and hit us at a different time, hoping to catch us off guard. That's why we're going into high mode once the sun goes down."

"What about all those cars out there?" Mickey asked.

"The only cars out there now are Treat's SUV and your truck. We made a great show of everyone driving off at three. They all went into town to their respective homes. Blackhorn can't possibly keep an eye on the house and see to it my agents stayed home. Even with help, he'd need a dozen or more people. With that many involved, someone would have heard about it."

"How did they get back here?" Mickey asked.

"They came in three cars and rendezvoused at the house in the woods. My people made their way back to the house in ones and twos using the woods to the west of us as cover. The two outside operatives made sure there was no one in the woods before allowing the people to sprint to the house. While it is possible Blackhorn knows how much firepower we've got, I'm hoping he wasn't close enough to see our people come back to the house. If there's no more questions, I'll be out in the foyer if you need me," O'Hara told them.

"I'll be in the kitchen," Denis said.

"Denis, is that wise?" Treat asked.

"Blackhorn doesn't give a shit about me. Besides, I've got a kitchen needing to be cleaned."

"He's right, Treat. Anyway, with the way he cooks, we have a vested interest in keeping him safe," O'Hara said, punching Denis lightly on his bicep.

Denis let O'Hara lead the way from the study. When O'Hara turned her back on him, he grabbed his bicep and mouthed "ouch" to Mickey and Treat.

O'Hara came back a few minutes later and gave them instructions on what they were to do for the rest of the evening.

As the evening wore on, Treat could feel the tension

mounting in the house. Treat and Mickey did as O'Hara told them—they stayed put in the study, kept the desk lamp between them and the windows, and kept the blinds down. The dogs stayed with them, curled up on the huge dog bed Denis had brought into the study for them, and fell asleep.

Treat and Mickey sat on the couch, holding hands and talking quietly.

"I'm so sorry I got you involved in this, Treat. I tried to stay away from you to protect you, but I couldn't. You're like a magnet."

Treat blushed at the compliment. She'd never been called a magnet before. "It's hardly your fault Blackhorn picked this time to put in an unwelcome appearance. Hell, we don't even know for sure it is Blackhorn. For all we know, it could be another one of the people you convicted. Or," Treat said with a smile, "it could be one of your many jilted lovers. Or the woman I saw you with the other day on your deck."

"Treat!" Mickey exclaimed with mock indignation. "I told you, you were the first since Grace."

"Darlin', I'm pulling your leg. I love seeing the fire in your eyes when you get all righteous," Treat said, laughing.

"Dammit, and I fall for it every time, don't I?" Mickey muttered.

"Yes, you do. That's what I love about you, baby."

"Do you?"

"Do I what?"

"Do you love me?"

Treat looked into Mickey's gray eyes. She realized she did indeed love the woman sitting next to her.

"I love you something awful, Mickey Heiden."

"Good, because I love you, too," Mickey said and leaned in to kiss Treat gently on the lips.

Treat put her hand on Mickey's cheek and kissed her back. They sat on the couch making out like a couple of teenagers, completely unaware of the passage of time or of the controlled chaos outside their door.

CHAPTER TWENTY-TWO

There was a light rap on the door and O'Hara stuck her head in.

"It's time," she said.

Treat and Mickey got up, turned off the lights, and followed by the dogs, headed for the stairs leading to Treat's bedroom. Only the foyer light was on downstairs. Treat felt a shot of adrenaline course through her system now that it was possible their lives could soon be in jeopardy.

O'Hara had told Treat to go about her bedtime routine as if nothing were wrong, with only a few minor changes. As they entered the bedroom, Treat turned on the light and immediately dimmed it so there was only ambient light. She lowered the shades on the four windows and then went into the bathroom and turned on the light there. She returned to the bedroom to find Mickey sitting on the bed with a puppy on either side of her.

"They know something's wrong," Mickey told her.

"I'll sit with them if you want to use the bathroom first," Treat said.

Mickey nodded and got up. Treat took her place between Bella and Lucy and murmured soothing "Mom" sounds as she stroked them. Bella was the first to relax. Lucy had her eyes on the bathroom door and wouldn't relax until Mickey returned.

When Mickey came back, the two women exchanged positions once again.

When Treat returned to the bedroom, she turned out the bathroom light. She found Mickey stretched out on the bed with a puppy snuggled into each armpit. It was postcard perfect.

Not wanting to disturb Mickey's sleep, she turned off the light as she'd been told to do and sat in the chair in the corner of the room. She was sure she would be unable to sleep.

Treat was unaware of how much time passed, but she was startled awake by a knock on her door. She realized as she struggled to wake up how deeply asleep she'd been. She got up and went to the door. She opened it to O'Hara.

"It's time," O'Hara said again.

"Okay," Treat told her.

This time, she had no choice but to awaken Mickey and the puppies. She touched Mickey lightly on the shoulder, hoping not to startle her.

"It's time, sweetie," she said as Mickey came awake.

The two women and their dogs left the bedroom as two OHS people took their place.

Mickey and Treat went into the guest bedroom farthest from the master bedroom. They slipped into bed and let the puppies crawl in between them.

"Only this once, girls," Mickey told Bella and Lucy as they settled down with deep sighs of contentment.

Mickey again slipped into a light sleep while Treat lay awake wondering if they would both be alive when the sun came up. She wondered if Blackhorn was dumb enough—or arrogant enough—to come after Mickey in Treat's home. He had to know she'd hired protection. A part of her wanted him to come after them because then Mickey would be free of the constant fear she faced every day. The other part of her didn't want Blackhorn anywhere near them because, while she had utmost faith in O'Hara and her team, the feds weren't treating the threat to their lives with the seriousness it warranted. Treat couldn't help but wonder why. If OHS failed, Mickey would be dead, and she knew she couldn't stand to lose her.

As these thoughts swirled through Treat's mind, her attention was drawn to how very quiet it had become. She wondered if another storm had moved into their area and if it was snowing outside. The two dogs got off the bed and headed for their own bed in the corner. Treat thought they must have gotten too warm sleeping between their humans. When the clock on the bedside table went dark, Treat didn't think anything of it. She'd been told that during blizzards, she'd lose electricity for anywhere from an hour to a full day. The clock had read 2:15. Treat felt Mickey snuggle into her back and put an arm over her to cup her breast. Thus, comforted by Mickey, Treat fell into a light sleep.

Treat came fully awake unsure where she was. The clock on the bedside table was blinking. She momentarily wondered whether the sound that had awakened her had been inside the house or part of a dream she couldn't now remember. It wasn't until she felt Mickey pull away from her back she knew Mickey had heard the sound, too. It was no dream.

Mickey reached into her backpack and came out with a weapon. "Stay here," Mickey whispered as she slid out of bed.

Treat, too, retrieved her own gun from the bedside table where she'd stashed it after the meeting with O'Hara that afternoon. She'd told O'Hara she had the weapon. She took the safety off as she moved around the bed.

"Please, Treat. Stay here with the girls. Let me check out what's going on. I'll be right back."

"All right, but if you're not back here in two minutes, I'm coming after you."

"I'll be back in less time than that," Mickey promised.

Treat knew the second she saw Mickey slip out the door it was a mistake letting her go out alone. She went to the door and slowly opened it. She snuck a quick look down the hallway before pulling her head back inside the room.

From that quick look, Treat knew two things. One was she had read too many mysteries, seen too many films, and knew she should be leaving this up to the professionals to handle. The second thing she knew for certain was there was something terribly wrong. The hallway was empty. If the sound were loud enough to awaken both her and Mickey, it would have been loud enough to waken the OHS team.

"Oh, shit," she muttered.

Treat opened the door a little wider and took another, longer look into the hallway. Nothing had changed. There was no one there. She stepped out of the bedroom. She pulled the door closed behind her to keep the dogs from following her. Her heart felt like it was hammering against her ribs. Ignoring it and hoping she wouldn't have a heart attack, she began easing her way down the hallway toward the stairs leading to the main floor of the house.

Treat froze when she heard a male voice say, "Bitch!"

"Bastard!" Mickey's voice answered.

Oh, my God, Blackhorn has Mickey, Treat's mind screamed. *He'll kill her if I don't do something. Anything.*

Treat still had the presence of mind to be cautious.

Keep him talking, Mickey, Treat silently pleaded. *Buy us both some time, baby.*

"Sheridan, you've got to give up this obsession with her," Jones said.

Jones? Treat's mind asked, shocked that Jones was in the room with Mickey and Blackhorn and God knew who else. *So, she really is a dirty agent. Dammit, Jones, come to your senses.*

Do your duty and save Mickey. Where are the two operatives who took our places in my bed? Has everyone turned tail and run on us?

"Shut up, Jones. No one told you to speak," Blackhorn snarled at her.

"Don't talk to me like that, Sheridan."

"Shut the fuck up, or I'll shut your big mouth for you!" Blackhorn yelled at her. "You stupid bitch—the only reason you're still alive is because you got me out of that hellhole prison. But if you don't shut up, I'll forget what you did for me."

"Sheridan, you don't mean that. We love each other. You told me that you loved me." Jones's voice had taken on a pleading tone.

Treat wasn't sure whether it was beginning to dawn on Jones that Blackhorn had lied to her or that her own stupidity in believing anything he had said to her had gotten her to this point.

"I would have told you anything you wanted to hear, you asshole, to get you to help me. Now either get out of here and save your skinny ass, or die right after she does," Blackhorn told Jones.

"You bastard," Jones growled at him.

Blackhorn laughed. "Don't even go for your weapon, Jonesy. You'll be dead before you get it out of your holster."

Treat had heard enough. She crept ever closer to the door, where a beam of light fell across the carpet. Once close to the door, she nudged it open a millimeter at a time. She peered into the well-lit room. Mickey was angled away from Treat, but Treat noted Mickey had blood running down the front of her T-shirt from a deep cut across her cheekbone. *The bastard hit her with his gun.*

Blackhorn stood about six feet away from Mickey,

holding his gun on her. He was a fireplug of a man—short and squat—dressed all in black with a black watch cap on his head. Treat knew she could have seen him numerous times and never noted his presence. As she watched him, he grabbed the watch cap from his head, revealing an awful attempt at dying his black hair, what there was of it, a deep auburn. There were smears of auburn on his bald spots and across his eyebrows. Confidence oozed from him. *He must think neither Mickey nor Jones are a threat.*

Treat glanced briefly at the bed and was shocked to see blood covering the head of the bed and up the wall behind it, and the bedspread was soaked in blood. From the amount of blood, both OHS people had to be dead.

Treat heard a soft groan, and her eyes were drawn to the figure lying on the floor in a growing pool of blood. It was O'Hara. Treat silently urged O'Hara to play possum so Blackhorn wouldn't try to finish the job of killing her.

"Jones, I'm not going to tell you again, get the hell out of here. I'm going to enjoy cutting this bitch to shreds a little at a time, and I don't want to have to worry about you," Blackhorn said. "Or stay and watch her die if you'd enjoy that, but don't try to stop me."

"Sheridan," Jones said.

Treat watched in horror as Blackhorn turned his gun on Jones and pulled the trigger. Jones collapsed in a heap, blood pumping from her chest. Jones struggled a moment, then became very, very still.

Treat raised her gun and pointed it at Blackhorn. With her foot, she pushed the door open. The movement caught his eye.

"Come on in, bitch," Blackhorn said, returning his eyes to Mickey. "I was wondering where you were. It'll be my pleasure to rid the world of one more useless bitch."

As Treat stepped into the room, Blackhorn turned his

head slowly toward Treat and at the same time brought his gun to bear on her. Treat saw he had another gun in his other hand—Mickey's gun—which he kept trained on Mickey. She held Blackhorn's piggish eyes with her own. His eyes were lifeless. She knew at that moment she was about to die if she didn't do something.

She fired twice. Blackhorn fell into a heap from well-placed shots within a few centimeters of each other and both in his heart. He'd been dead before he hit the ground. Treat managed to get her finger off the trigger of her gun and lower the weapon to her side.

Mickey rushed to her and grabbed her in a hug so tight Treat could barely breathe. "When I saw what he'd done to your beautiful face, I knew I wanted him dead," Treat said. "I'm so sorry there was no one here to protect you, baby."

"You came to my rescue. You're my knight in shining armor," Mickey said, wincing from the pain in her cheek. "Can't smile."

"I wasn't about to lose you, my love, now that I've finally found you."

When Mickey let her go, Treat went to O'Hara's side.

"She's still breathing," Treat whispered as she put her hand on O'Hara's chest to try to stop the bleeding. "Thank God."

Mickey went to Jones's side and put a finger on the artery in her neck. "She's dead."

Treat's world began spinning on its axis again. The first thing Treat noticed was the smell of death—blood, feces, and urine—hanging oppressively in the air. She thought for a moment she was going to throw up but managed to push the bile in her throat down. She watched as Mickey went to the two people who were in their bed and put her fingers on their necks. They were both dead as well.

CHAPTER TWENTY-THREE

Without thinking about what she was doing, Treat made a quick count. There were four dead in her bedroom, one seriously wounded, and another needing stitches. Her mind started repeating over and over. *Please let Denis be alive. Please let Denis be alive. And what about the other OHS people? Did Blackhorn kill them, too?*

As if her prayers were being answered, Denis, with two OHS people on his heels, charged into the room. Denis looked around the room, pulled out his cell phone, and speed-dialed a number. He told whoever was on the other end of the phone to send an ambulance because there were at least four dead and a severely wounded security agent. After he snapped the phone shut, he went to O'Hara and knelt by her side.

"Let me see," he told Treat as he gently nudged her away. "Bring me a towel."

Mickey sped into the bathroom, returning with a large white towel. Denis unbuttoned O'Hara's blouse and exposed a hole in her upper left chest. He put the towel on the hole and pressed down.

"You'd best live, O'Hara," he whispered to her. "We're business partners, and business partners are not allowed to die on the opening day of business."

Denis turned to Treat and Mickey. "You two go downstairs. The local and state cops are on their way in. They should be coming up the driveway as we speak. Drink heavily sweetened tea. I don't want either of you going into shock."

Treat heard the dogs whining behind the closed door of the guest room. She made it into the hallway, and as she turned toward the guest room, her knees gave out, and she sat down hard before Mickey, who was right behind her, could catch her.

Mickey got Treat to her feet and led her to the staircase. Treat's feet felt like lead, and her knees had turned to jelly as she wobbled toward the stairs clinging to Mickey.

By the time they reached the foyer, the Brattleboro Police, the Vermont State Police, the emergency medical services, and several cars that could only be the feds were screaming up to the house.

Mickey opened the door to the late-arriving authorities and pointed up the staircase. The police raced up the staircase followed by the paramedics and a whole lot of other people. Treat didn't know who they were or what their purpose was, nor did she care. She went into the kitchen and struggled into one of the tall chairs at the table in front of the kitchen window. Her mind was immobilized, unable to get around what had just happened upstairs in her bedroom. She dropped her head into her hands to try to find a way to get her mind to work again. She heard Mickey enter the kitchen, put the heat on beneath the teakettle, and then get herself a soft drink from the fridge. Treat glanced up and saw Mickey hold the cold can to the cut on her face to staunch the oozing wound.

"There's ice cubes in the freezer. They may work better. Better yet, get an EMT to look at the cut," Treat said.

Mickey didn't say anything, but went to the freezer and

removed the container of ice cubes. She dropped a dozen cubes onto a kitchen towel and held it to the cut.

While Mickey was busy getting the drinks and trying to stop the bleeding, Treat sat staring out the window without seeing anything. She was brought back to the moment when Mickey set a steaming cup of tea in front of her.

"I've put lots of sugar in it, so it's going to be very sweet. You need to drink it fast so you can get some sugar into your system."

Denis came into the kitchen and asked, "How about you, Mickey, can I fix you a cup as well?"

"No, thanks, Denis. I'll get my jolt from this," Mickey said, holding up her can of soda.

Two men slammed into the kitchen at the same time and began asking questions as they talked over each other in order to gain ascendancy. Finally, they ground to a halt when they realized Mickey had walked out of the kitchen. Denis was fixing himself a cup of tea, and Treat had turned her back to them.

"Lady," the man in the gray suit said in a threatening tone.

"Who are you?" Treat wanted to know.

"Pardon me, ma'am," the older of the two men said. "My name is Lou Gerrick. I'm chief of police in Brattleboro."

"Tell me what happened," the other man demanded without introducing himself.

He could only be a fed, Treat decided.

Treat's mind finally fully engaged as her temper flared. "Look, asshole, I just witnessed a psychopath, whom you allowed to escape from your prison, slaughter a woman in cold blood, and who then pointed his gun at my head. To make matters worse, he severely wounded my bodyguard and hit my lover in the face with his gun. All the while, there were only two FBI agents on the scene, and one was the psychopath's accomplice. Why is that? Chief, I'd be asking your friend here that same question if I were you. In any event, do not give me one iota of shit," Treat told the fed in no uncertain terms. "Now, either tell me who you are or get the fuck out of my kitchen."

"Listen, lady, I can have you arrested for obstruction of justice," the unknown man threatened.

"Oh, for God's sake, Ben. The woman told you what happened. You should have listened to what she was saying. Stop being a pain in the ass and introduce yourself," Mickey said from the doorway.

"My name is Benjamin Stern. I'm with the FBI, and since Blackhorn is a federal prisoner, we have jurisdiction."

CHAPTER TWENTY-FOUR

After Miriam LoPelasco, Treat's attorney, arrived, Gerrick and Stern spent an hour and a half questioning Treat on what happened in the master bedroom, what she knew of Blackhorn, how he had ended up in her bedroom, who shot O'Hara, who shot Jones, and who shot Blackhorn. After they finished asking those questions, they asked them all again.

Before they could ask the questions a third time, Miriam said, "That's enough. Any follow-up questions you may have you can send to me, and I'll ensure you get a response."

Stern started to protest Miriam's directive, but Gerrick muttered, "Give it a rest." Both men got up with deep sighs and left Miriam and Treat alone together. It was a relief to have it over. Stern and the chief still had to interview Mickey and probably Denis, though.

"When do you plan on leaving my client's home?" Miriam asked.

"We'll leave when we're through here," Stern said.

Miriam merely looked at him.

"We'll return custody of Ms. Dandridge's home to her as soon as possible." Stern amended his first answer.

"I'm sure you can find out exactly when that will be, Agent Stern, and let me know as soon as possible."

Agent Stern wasn't able to best Miriam, so he merely nodded.

"These are the most comfortable chairs I've ever sat in," Miriam said after the two men left the room. "Where did you get them?"

"In town. If you'll stay a day or two, I'll take you to see them," Treat said, wondering how Miriam could talk about such a mundane matter after she'd heard what had happened upstairs.

"How in the world did you get yourself involved in all this?" Miriam wanted to know.

"I didn't get involved in this," Treat responded. "I got involved with Mickey."

"Is it serious?" Miriam asked.

"This thing with Mickey?" Miriam merely raised an eyebrow at her. "It could be," Treat told her honestly.

"I hope you know a therapist here," Miriam said.

"No, I don't. Presumably, since you brought it up, you do," Treat said, smiling. "Why do you ask?"

"As a matter of fact, I made a few phone calls on my way up here. The one name that came up over and over is Catherine Standish."

"So, what makes you think I'm going to need Catherine Standish?"

"Oh, come on, Treat. You saw a woman brutally murdered, your lover's life was in danger, and a maniac was willing to murder you, too. Let's not even mention the six other people Blackhorn killed. And let's not say anything about your bodyguard whom he tried to kill as well. And then you shot the psychopath. If you think either you or Mickey will be unaffected by all that, you are seriously deluding yourself," she said emphatically.

"Okay. You've made your point. I'll call her."

Denis came into the room and asked if they needed anything.

"Tell me where Mickey is," Treat said.

"She's on the couch in your office, and yes, the girls are with her."

"Presumably, the girls are the Lab youngsters I saw outside?" Miriam asked.

"They would be the girls," Denis told her.

"You guys have matching puppies?"

"Yes and no. Mickey got her Lucy first. I fell head over heels in love with her, so Mickey gave me Bella," Treat said.

"Oh, God, you two are too, too precious already," Miriam said, laughing.

"Do me a favor, Miriam?" Treat asked.

"Of course, Treat. You know that," Miriam said.

"Sit in on Mickey and Denis's session with the boys," Treat told her. "Add the charges to my bill. We'll put you up here tonight if we have to stay here, and I'm sure Denis will fix you one of his fabulous meals."

"Done. And not because you asked or because you'll pay me, but because it's been too long since I've had one of Denis's meals," she told Treat.

Treat laughed at her while Denis beamed.

Miriam turned to Denis and asked, "Mexican, Denis? Please!"

"Absolutely," Denis told her. "I think I've got everything I need," he muttered distractedly as he left the room.

"Uh-oh," Miriam murmured. "It's time I go earn my dinner."

Treat looked into the foyer and saw Gerrick and Stern conferring.

"Mind if I invite the chief to dinner, Treat?" Miriam asked as she approached the doors to the foyer.

"Not at all," Treat told her. "It never hurts to have the chief of police dining at your table."

Chapter Twenty-five

After a late lunch where Mickey said next to nothing and the others carried on conversations around her, Lou said he had to go to the police station to complete the paperwork on what he called "this fiasco."

Miriam walked him out. When she returned, she said, "Lou says we're about to be inundated with the media. He can no longer justify having officers out at the road to keep them off your property."

"Is there anything we can do to keep them out?" Treat wanted to know. "At least long enough for us to sneak off to the house in the woods."

"I'll go out and talk to them to see if I can't threaten them with terrible harm if they don't stay off your property, but I know that doesn't always work with big-city journalists. But we'll see."

Sure enough, no sooner had the chief and his team departed Treat's property than the media came swarming up her driveway looking quite like locusts come to plunder the land.

After talking to the journalists, Miriam returned to the kitchen where the others were gathered. She said, "I don't think we've seen the last of the reporters. As soon as they're told to get the story or else, they'll be back at the door. As much as I hate to say this, I think we need to leave the house sooner rather than later."

"Where do we go? We can't go to Mickey's house," Treat said. "Nor can we go to Denis's house, there's no furniture there yet."

"Denis's house? Does that mean you're staying here?" Mickey wanted to know.

"It does," Denis said.

"I'm really glad."

"Why don't we go to Boston? And stay there while the furor dies down and we get this place cleaned up?" Denis asked.

"Boston would be fine with me. How about you, Mickey? Fancy spending some time in Boston?" Treat asked.

"Whatever," Mickey replied listlessly.

"Where would we stay?" Treat asked Denis. "There can't be that many hotels that will accept pets, and I don't think it's a good idea to leave the girls in a kennel right now. They're too freaked out, and if we abandon them now, they may never recover."

"I have to confess I've been looking at property in Boston since I got here," Denis told her.

"Find anything interesting?"

"I did indeed. There's a condo conversion of a home built in 1873. I've been talking to the listing agent, who told me the condo is twenty-three hundred square feet with three bedrooms and three baths. It's located across the street from Boston Commons."

"Sounds fabulous," Treat told him. "How is that going to help us find some place to stay now?"

"I think I can help," Miriam said. "Denis, can you get me the listing agent's name and number?"

"Of course."

"Let's take the girls out," Treat said to Mickey, knowing there was nothing either of them could do to help in finding housing for the night.

"Hang on and let me check around out back. Some of those reporters may have slipped onto the property," said Sam, one of O'Hara's people.

Treat had completely forgotten about Sam. She'd been standing quietly looking out the door since they'd come into the kitchen. *Talk about melding into the woodwork!* Treat thought.

Sam stepped outside to look for reporters.

"Are you okay?" Treat asked Mickey.

Mickey gave her a withering look.

"Okay, let me rephrase that. How are you doing?"

"About as well as can be expected after having a gun pointed at your head, having six people killed by a psychopath who was gunning for me, and not having anywhere to live," Mickey said bitterly.

"You have somewhere to live, Mickey," Treat said quietly.

"We haven't talked about being a couple yet, Treat, much less about living together," Mickey said.

"Maybe we should have that conversation, then," Treat said. "In the meantime, though, consider the time in Boston as an extended sleepover."

That got a wisp of a smile from Mickey. "Treat, I'm afraid I'm so messed up right now I wouldn't make anyone a good partner," Mickey told her honestly.

"Then get some help, Mickey," Treat said as gently as she could. "I want you in my life. I love you."

"Yeah?" Mickey asked with the first genuine smile Treat had seen from her in days.

"I don't want to be out on that limb by myself," Treat responded with a smile of her own. "And don't you think it's time I start calling you by your real name, by the way?"

"I don't care what you call me as long as you call me," Mickey said, laughing at herself for using a tired old cliché. "Actually, I'd like it if you'd continue to call me Mickey. I've come to like the name."

"I can do that. Getting used to saying 'Jo' would take some time and could prove to be awkward."

It was at that moment Sam stepped back into the kitchen, "No reporters that I could see," she announced.

"Let's let the girls do their thing," Mickey said, opening the door for Bella and Lucy, who, of course, dashed outside.

Treat knew Mickey was avoiding agreeing to seek therapy. She wondered if the conversation about living together would ever be completed. In her heart, she knew it would be a while before they returned to the topic of living together because Mickey was right. She was messed up, and as long as she refused to seek help, she'd never be able to heal. *You're not doing much better than she is.*

Treat and Mickey returned to the warm house, followed immediately by the dogs. They all went into the kitchen where it was cozy. Denis had somehow managed to bake something that smelled like cinnamon rolls.

Miriam reappeared at the kitchen door with a huge grin on her face.

"We have a deal," Miriam said.

"Great!" Treat said, relieved they'd have somewhere to stay. "When can we leave for Boston?"

"After dark, assuming I can get this thing organized," Denis said, looking up from a list he was making.

"Another thing, what is Stevens still doing here?"

"Oh, she resigned from the Bureau and joined our team. For the foreseeable future, she and Sam will be our primary security team, augmented on an as-needed basis by the other team members," Denis said.

CHAPTER TWENTY-SIX

Treat, Mickey, Denis, Sam, and Stevens stayed in Boston for nearly six months, celebrating both Thanksgiving and Christmas there. Denis and Treat had fun buying furniture for both the Boston condo and Denis's house in Guilford.

In Brattleboro, they had attended the funerals of the members of Treat's security team. Treat was able to assure their families they would be taken care of. Treat had also visited O'Hara and spoken with her nearly every day to find out how she was doing. The doctors had told O'Hara it was looking better for a full recovery if she stayed focused on her rehabilitation program.

O'Hara had been released from the hospital but had been told she could not return to work until she finished rehabilitation. Mickey and O'Hara compared detailed notes on their respective rehab programs. Denis and Treat were too squeamish to sit in on those sessions after they'd heard the first one.

Treat had made an appointment to see Catherine Standish, the therapist Miriam had recommended. Catherine was a woman in her late forties. She had salt-and-pepper hair and was slim and easy on the eyes. Her office was in one of the old Victorian homes lining the main street into Brattleboro that had been converted into small intimate offices. Treat liked the woman a lot. She was easy to talk to, had an easy laugh, and prodded Treat gently but firmly with her questions.

When they returned to the Guilford house, it was with a great deal of trepidation that Treat went upstairs to her bedroom. Not only had Denis made sure the room was clean and had new carpet, but he had replaced all the furnishings as well. With the new furniture, a fresh coat of paint, and new carpet, it looked like an entirely different room, but Mickey said she couldn't sleep there. So they slept in the bedroom across the hall. Treat hoped they could move back into the master bedroom sooner rather than much later.

Two weeks after they returned to Guilford, a special delivery letter arrived for Mickey. The Marine Corps was recalling her to active duty. She was to report to JAG headquarters in Washington DC in three days.

Before Mickey left for DC the first time, Treat told Mickey she was concerned about Mickey's unwillingness to see a therapist to help her deal with the fallout of Blackhorn's attack on her. Previously when Treat brought up the topic of therapy, Mickey had bristled. This time, though, she was downright belligerent.

"You're beginning to sound like a goddamned broken record, Treat," Mickey said sitting up. "Just because you can't handle the aftermath doesn't mean I can't. Stop nagging me about a fucking therapist. I don't need one."

"When's the last time you slept for eight straight hours?" Treat asked patiently.

"I haven't slept for eight hours a night since I was ten," Mickey said.

"When's the last time you didn't dream about either Blackhorn pointing the gun at you or Jones's death?"

"What's that got to do with anything? It'll go away on its

own without some goddamned shrink messing with my head," Mickey said angrily and stomped out of the room.

Treat was surprised at Mickey's attitude and refusal to see a therapist. She didn't know what the reasons were, but whatever they were, she knew they would eventually jeopardize their relationship if she didn't get help. She wondered how many times they would have that same conversation. Or how many times she'd be willing to have the conversation with Mickey before she finally gave up and quit pushing. She didn't have a definite answer for either question. She knew, however, Mickey was right about one thing, she was sounding like a broken record, and she was tired of doing that.

After Mickey left for DC the next day, Treat was sitting on the patio watching the dogs explore their territory. The trees were beginning to change to their spring colors, daffodils and crocuses were blooming everywhere, and the temperature was on the rise.

O'Hara came out the kitchen door with a mug in her hand. "Have you got a minute?"

"Sure. But I have a question to ask."

"Okay, shoot."

"When will mud season be over?"

O'Hara laughed. "Soon. The ground will get more and more solid as the sun warms and begins drying it out."

"Thank God. What did you need to tell me?"

"I've received the investigative report on the shootings. I thought you should know neither Jones's nor Mickey's gun was fired. The bullets found in Blackhorn match your gun. None of the law enforcement agencies plan on doing anything with that piece of information. They've all chalked it up to self-defense."

"Damn," Treat whispered.

While she knew she'd killed Blackhorn, she'd been too

busy dealing with the nightmares and Mickey to give it much thought. It was Catherine who brought up the fact she'd killed a man. As she talked to Catherine about how she felt, she knew she could live with having killed Sheridan Blackhorn and would have no nightmares, no regrets about having done so.

"Are you okay with this?" O'Hara wanted to know.

"Yes. Yes, I am. Thanks for telling me."

Chapter Twenty-seven

Mickey's first visit home from Washington DC had been strained, much to Treat's chagrin. Now Mickey was coming home again. Treat was leaning against the maple tree near the front door waiting for Mickey, who had called from the freeway exit. When Mickey pulled into the driveway, Treat's heart began beating faster.

Mickey exited her truck and paused. Treat could feel Mickey's eyes scanning her, but something was different in a major way. There was no heat in Mickey's eyes. But there was something else.

"You've cut your hair!" Treat exclaimed.

After the murders, Mickey had let her hair grow out. It turned out she had naturally curly hair, and Treat had loved running her fingers through those soft curls.

"Yeah, the Corps frowned on my mane. I had to get it cut to military standards. Do you still love me?"

"I do, Samson, I do."

"Then why, Delilah, are we standing in the driveway when there's a perfectly good bed upstairs?"

"Why indeed."

But lovemaking was not to be in their immediate future. Treat wasn't sure Mickey hadn't just been bantering about making love. They hadn't made love in an age, nor did they make love that weekend either.

On a Sunday morning three weeks later, as Mickey prepared to return to DC after another tense weekend at home, Treat handed her a slip of paper with a name and telephone number on it.

"What's this?" Mickey asked.

"The name of a therapist in DC, compliments of Catherine."

"Treat, you're really pissing me off about this. I've told you I don't need a therapist."

"Mickey, my love, you're lying to yourself if you think you don't need to talk to someone."

"You don't know what you're talking about," Mickey said. "You need to mind your own fucking business."

"I thought you were my business. If you can honestly tell me you sleep more than three or four hours a night, I'll leave you alone about this. If last night is any indication of how well you sleep, you are on your way to a nervous breakdown."

"What do you mean? I slept fine last night."

"You were having nightmares practically from the moment you fell asleep. You finally got up at two thirty and didn't come back to bed until five. You call that a good night's sleep?"

"I've got to go. I need to be back in DC before nightfall."

Treat knew that by leaving now, Mickey would be in DC by two in the afternoon, but didn't say anything.

It was another month before Mickey returned to Vermont.

"I've started seeing your therapist," Mickey said as they got ready for bed her first night back.

"She's not my therapist, she's yours. What do you think about her?"

"I like her. I don't feel any judgment or expectations from her."

Treat wondered if what Mickey had left unspoken was "like I do from you." *Probably.*

After Mickey started seeing her therapist, they returned to seeing each other two or three times each month with either Treat traveling to DC or Mickey returning to Vermont. Mickey admitted she really missed Vermont and preferred returning to Brattleboro rather than have Treat travel to DC.

The following Wednesday, Denis made them a late-night cup of hot chocolate. "O'Hara's moved back to her apartment in town," Denis said.

"She told me," Treat said, wondering where this conversation was headed.

"Now that OHS is no longer occupying the house in the woods, I was thinking of moving out there. Will it be a problem?" Denis asked.

"Well, I had the place built for you, so it would only make sense you would occupy it. Why?"

"I've been thinking I need my own space. I think the time is right for me to move out there."

"Makes sense. Are you going to tell me why?"

"Why?" Denis asked.

"Who is he?"

"Damn, am I that transparent?" Denis asked.

"No. It's that I know you so well. Now tell me."

"We've been seeing one another occasionally. Each time I see him, I find myself not wanting the evening to end, and I can't wait to see him again," Denis confessed.

"Who is he?"

"Promise me you won't laugh."

"I promise I won't laugh, Denis."

"Okay. He owns his own business here in Guilford. I met him one afternoon at Walker Gardens out near Putney. He's not gorgeous in the blond-blue-eyed tradition, but I love looking at him."

"What kind of business does he own, boyfriend?" Treat asked.

"This is where you cannot laugh. Promise?"

Treat nodded that she wouldn't laugh.

"He owns a composting business. He makes and sells organic compost. He only has to work three seasons, and he makes a very good living at it. He has the most fabulous hands, Treat."

True to her word, Treat didn't laugh. It was a struggle, but she managed to keep the laugh that was fighting to emerge contained. She needed to change the subject.

"Okay, we're about to reach the point of too much information, Denis," Treat said. "When do I get to meet him and what is the man's name?"

"I thought I'd invite him to Sunday dinner. I'd like to show him the house in the trees as well as your supposed gardens and see what he thinks we should do with them."

"Invite him for Saturday. Mickey will be here," Treat said.

"Okay. We can do that. His name is Robin. People call him Rob. Treat, I hope you like him."

"He sounds wonderful, Denis. I know if he's stolen your heart, I'll like him for sure. I'm so glad you've met someone you want to spend time with, Denis. You deserve someone to love who will love you back."

"Thank you. I think he's the one."

Lucy and Bella were back and ready to come inside. They all went to bed. Treat dreamed of holding Mickey all night and slept like a baby.

CHAPTER TWENTY-EIGHT

Treat was awakened very early that Saturday morning when Mickey slid into the bed, Treat mumbled sleepily, "Hey, girlfriend," and rolled over onto her side, facing away from Mickey. Mickey pressed herself against Treat's warm back, put an arm over Treat, and cupped her breast.

Within a few moments, both women and their dogs were deeply asleep.

The next morning, everyone in the house was up, showered, and dressed by eight. Denis fixed them waffles and had fresh strawberries and mangos as well.

"Been assigned any interesting cases?" Denis asked.

"No. They're all boring as watching golf on television. Anything interesting happen here?" Mickey asked.

"I need to go out to the house," Denis said, avoiding answering Mickey. "Then I need to do some grocery shopping. We'll be eating at seven this evening."

He left the two women sitting at the counter.

"What is that about?" Mickey asked.

"He's spent the last three days cleaning the house in the woods."

"Why?"

"We're having a special guest for dinner, and Denis wants to show him the house."

"How special?"

"So special that Denis has been in a dither all week. I've never seen him this nervous or this excited about anyone he's dated."

"Is there love in the air?" Mickey asked.

Before Treat could answer her, Denis returned to the kitchen. "Can I see you for a minute, Treat?"

"Of course."

They went into the living room, leaving Mickey in the kitchen with O'Hara, who had arrived a few minutes earlier.

"I've invited O'Hara and her new girlfriend to eat with us this evening. I hope you don't mind," he said.

"Of course not, Denis. Besides, it's your party, you get to invite whomever you choose," she paused. "O'Hara has a girlfriend?"

"She's seeing one of her nurses from the hospital. A woman named, of all things, Elsie."

"Wow. Well, it should be good fun," Treat said.

"Um, I'm not through with the surprises. Miriam and Lou will also be here."

"Sounds like we're having our first real dinner party," Treat said, laughing.

"It does, and if I don't get a move on, we'll be eating take-out pizza," Denis said, laughing in turn.

"That wouldn't be the worst thing that could happen," Treat said.

"Bite your tongue, Treat Dandridge. We are not having pizza for the first meal I cook for Rob!" Denis said, aghast at the very thought.

Treat laughed at the look on his face. "Is there anything Mickey and I can do while you're gone?" she asked.

"Yes. Go shopping."

"Denis, are you saying Mickey and I cannot be trusted in your clean house?" Treat said.

"Yes. I'm serious, Treat. Please try not to mess the house up."

"I'm resisting the urge to go from room to room knocking things over, throwing pillows on the floor, and tracking mud in from the garden," Treat told him.

"You're trying to give me a heart attack," Denis said, dramatically clutching his chest.

"Relax, boyfriend. Mickey and I will go to Keene. I want to go to the Toadstool Bookstore," Treat said, letting him off the hook.

When they had returned from Keene, they parked at the head of the driveway. Mickey grabbed the bags from the bookstore, leaving the bag with a colander and knife from the Kitchen Store for Treat.

"You're going to be in so much trouble, Treat. Denis is going to have a conniption because you're bringing in yet another colander. You go in first. That way the fireworks will have died down by the time I get inside. In fact, if you'll let the girls out, we'll go around back. Crawl on out when you're able," Mickey told Treat as she handed the shopping bags to her.

"Yeah, yuk it up. But I am making a note my lean, mean fighting machine of a Marine is afraid of my gay housekeeper," Treated taunted.

O'Hara and Sam both laughed out loud at the image of Mickey being afraid of anything, let alone Denis.

"I'm not afraid of a wussy housekeeper," Mickey shot back.

"Who are you calling wussy?" Denis asked from the front steps.

Treat laughed again when Mickey jumped a foot at the sound of his voice.

"Lucy," Mickey said.

"O'Hara," Treat said at the same time.

"Hey!" O'Hara protested. "Don't put me in the middle of this fiasco. I want to eat this evening."

"I wondered why it was taking you so long to come into the house. Treat, what have you done?" Denis asked as he came down the steps to take a couple of the bags from her.

"Me?" Treat asked feigning innocence. "I haven't done anything. Mickey bought another colander, though. I tried to dissuade her, but noooo. She insisted we needed another colander. She really wouldn't listen to me."

Everyone laughed at the look on Mickey's face. She couldn't believe Treat was trying to blame her for the lime-green colander.

"Denis, just remember who brought the other eight colanders home," Mickey said, laughing.

"Okay, Treat. You and the new colander may as well come in," Denis told her smiling. "Lime green? Girlfriend, you have totally lost your fashion sense since you moved here!"

"I'll be around back with the girls," Mickey said.

"I'll be out soon," Treat said, and added, "I hope."

"Denis," Treat said, "the gardener you hired has done a wonderful job of restoring the beds the media ruined. Are you working with him on doing something out back?"

"Actually, Rob and I and the gardener have a plan. We're going to create several raised beds on the side of the house for vegetables and cut flowers. Spring will be spectacular," Denis said.

Denis led the way into the house and to the kitchen. Once there, Treat pulled her latest treasure from the Kitchen Store bag. After a minute of staring at it, a small smile appeared at the corners of Denis's mouth.

"I hate to admit it, Treat, but it's kind of pretty, and it does add a touch of color to an otherwise mundane kitchen décor."

"Ha!" Treat exclaimed in triumph. "I knew you'd end up liking it. Look what I got you."

She slowly and dramatically pulled out the kitchen knife he had coveted for so long.

"Oh. My. God," Denis exclaimed, emphasizing each word. "You found it! I've wanted one of these for years!"

"You are the only person I know who gets orgasmic over a kitchen utensil," Treat said, laughing.

"This is no ordinary knife. This is a *yanagi* knife made of blue carbon steel and is *kasumi aoko* grade. It is a work of art," he explained to her.

"Then we should hang it on the wall in the living room," Treat said. "It's still only a knife, Denis. A kitchen knife, at that. I can use it to open Amazon boxes."

Treat was sure he had visibly paled at the thought of his precious knife being used to open an ordinary mailing box.

"Out! Out! My knife and I have a dinner to prepare!" he told her as he shooed her out the kitchen door onto the patio.

She laughed but allowed herself to be pushed out of doors where she joined Mickey and the girls.

"Was Denis aghast at the colander?" Mickey asked as Treat settled onto the chaise lounge next to hers.

"He actually took it quite well. And he was ecstatic about the knife," Treat said.

"I'm glad you came out here with me, baby," Mickey said.

The almost-warm sun worked its magic on the two women as they lapsed into a comfortable silence. Treat watched the girls chasing the first of the summer's butterflies and hop across the grass as the occasional grasshopper tried to get out of their way.

"Treat, it's time to get ready for dinner," Denis said as he gently shook her foot.

"Damn, I must have dozed off," Treat said.

Treat looked over at the chaise lounge next to hers expecting to see Mickey asleep there, but it was empty.

"Where's Mickey?"

"She's already upstairs."

Treat reached down between her legs to stroke the velvety soft ears of Bella, who had, unbeknownst to Treat, crawled up on the chaise to nap with her. Bella was instantaneously awake. Treat stood up and stretched the kinks out of her back. She folded the light blanket someone had put over her as she slept. She looked around her property, still awed by its beauty and thinking how lucky she was to live in Vermont.

"Get a move on it, Treat," Denis called from the kitchen door. "Dinner will wait for no woman."

"I'm coming, I'm coming," she muttered as she moved toward the kitchen door.

CHAPTER TWENTY-NINE

Six months later, Treat came out of her office and went in search of Denis. It was the one-year anniversary of the murders, and she knew she didn't want to spend the day cooped up in her office. Of course, she wished Mickey could be with her to comfort her and be comforted by her. Mickey wasn't able to come home this weekend, so Denis would have to suffice. *Damn, it's hard loving a Marine.* She admitted it was getting harder and harder to say good-bye to Mickey at the end of those weekends when she came home.

She couldn't find Denis in the house, so she went outside to look for him. It was a rare warm late fall day for New England. Treat looked across the meadow to the woods. The trees had lost their stunning fall foliage and now stood bare. The grass in the meadow was turning brown. There was beauty in the starkness of the soon-to-be winter landscape, she decided. She found Denis working in one of his raised flower beds. She knew from what he had told her the night before the bed needed to be turned and some of Rob's compost had to be worked into the soil before Denis could plant the bulbs—crocuses, dahlias, tulips, and daffodils—that would bloom the following spring. The girls were nearby playing in the spray from a hose Denis had put a sprinkler on for the dogs' enjoyment.

As Treat approached the bed, Denis stepped out and picked up another hose from the ground. He sprayed both dogs, much to their delight. It was hilarious watching the dogs trying to bite the water as it sprayed from the nozzle. He turned to spray the bed and caught Treat full in the face.

"Oops. Sorry," he said.

Treat knew he wasn't sorry at all. Indeed, she knew it hadn't been an accident either. She said nothing. Instead, she walked over and picked up the second hose, removed the sprinkler, and sprayed him right back. The battle was enjoined. The dogs joined in the melee but backed away after the two humans stepped into the flower bed. Before anyone could count to five, mud was flying. Treat accidentally on purpose bumped into Denis which, because of the slippery mud, caused him to fall down. While Treat was laughing uproariously at Denis, he grabbed one of her ankles and gave it a good yank. She was literally swept off her feet and fell into the mud next to him.

The battle raged on. By the time Denis called "uncle," they were both covered in mud from the tops of their heads to the bottoms of their feet. Somewhere in the morass was one of Treat's sandals and Denis's Boston Red Sox baseball cap. Neither wanted to dig around to find either the sandal or the cap, so they became part of the compost and dirt.

As she stepped out of the bed, Treat wished Mickey had been present even though she suspected she would have retreated from the fight. It still would have been fun to spray her with water to see what she would have done. Maybe she would have surprised Treat and joined in the fun. She realized the battle had lifted her spirits a little.

"Where'd you go, girlfriend?" Denis asked as he tried to scrape some of the mud off his legs.

"I was wishing Mickey were here," she said. "I love you,

Denis, really I do. But when I realized that today is the one-year anniversary of the murders, I didn't want to be holed up in the house alone. What I wanted was for Mickey to be here, too. Having a long-distance relationship is not as easy as I thought—or hoped—it would be."

"I wouldn't think so," Denis told her sympathetically. "Is she coming home this weekend?"

"No, she's got a trial starting in a couple of weeks and needed to do some preliminary interviews," Treat said, not happy.

"Here, let me rinse you off, girlfriend," he said as he turned the hose on her one more time.

Denis got most of the mud off her and her clothes, but she was soaked to the skin.

"I'm going to go take a shower. How about you?" Denis asked.

"I think I'll dry off out here first. The guys down at the Guilford Country Store are telling me this weather won't hold and winter will arrive very soon," she informed Denis. "I want to catch as much sun as I can while it's here."

"Oh, good," Denis said sarcastically. "I can hardly wait for the freezing temps to return."

"Wussy," she teased him.

"Harrumph," was his response.

As Treat turned toward the house, she noticed O'Hara and Sam were sitting on the patio and had seen the mud fight. They waved merrily and disappeared into the house.

Treat watched Denis return to the house and thought how lucky she was he had decided to stay in Guilford with her—well, not exactly with her. He and Rob lived out in the house in the woods but had their meals with her. Their company had been a godsend with Mickey gone so much of the time over the last six months.

Once Denis disappeared into the house, Treat moved away from the sodden ground near the flower bed and sat down on the grass. The smell of newly mown grass lingered in the air. She lay back so all her clothes would dry. Within seconds, the dogs were stretched out on either side of her and had already fallen asleep. The sun wasn't hot by any stretch of the imagination, but it was warm enough to put her to sleep.

Treat awoke with a start, her heart pounding. Someone was standing over her. At first, she couldn't tell who it was because the person was standing with the sun behind him and Treat couldn't make out any features. Even after a year, her first thought was that it was Blackhorn standing over her. The fear that coursed through her body was powerful enough to feel like a blow.

Treat jumped to her feet. The adrenaline that had poured into her bloodstream began to dissipate when she realized it was Mickey standing nearby. *God, she's beautiful! I'm so happy she's in my life.* Mickey wore a pair of Levi's, a pale blue long-sleeved T-shirt that showed off the fact she'd been working out, and a pair of old Timberland boots. *The woman couldn't be any more sexy if she tried.*

"What are you doing here? You said you couldn't come up this weekend," Treat said as her words tumbled out all at once.

"Sweetie, come over and sit down, and I'll tell you why I'm here this weekend," Mickey told her, leading the way to the rockers on the patio.

"First of all, are you okay?" Treat asked.

"Yes, I'm okay."

"Thank God! Okay, tell me why you're here."

"I have lots to tell you. When I left my office last evening, I looked at the calendar and realized today was the anniversary of the killings. I knew, too, I had to be with you. I got here as fast as I could. I've been working hard with my therapist. I know I haven't talked about it a lot, but I've begun to feel the difference. I can sleep the entire night now. I can talk about how scared I was. I've begun to feel less helpless and less guilty about my fears."

Mickey stopped because she'd run out of breath. She glanced at Treat.

Treat smiled at her, hoping to encourage her to continue.

Mickey took a deep breath, and began again. "Four months ago, I began to understand I was no longer happy being in the Marine Corps. I love the Corps and always will. But, Treat, I love you more. I need you. I need you in my life full-time. I need to be able to hold you and be held by you. I need to have a full-time relationship, with everything that entails—the ups and the downs—with you. I want you and I need you. Two weeks ago, I got orders for a thirteen-month assignment in Japan. It was the impetus I needed. I put in my retirement papers. They've given me a medical retirement because I was wounded in the line of duty and suffered from post-traumatic stress disorder after the ordeal with Blackhorn here."

"Oh, my God, Mickey. Really? That's wonderful! Are you sure you want to leave the Corps? It's been your home for so many years. Can you leave it? When will you come home permanently?"

"I'm very sure of this decision. If you still want me in your life, I'm yours. The retirement ceremony was yesterday morning. My stuff was picked up by the moving company in the afternoon."

"Of course I want you. In so many ways."

Mickey stood up and knelt on one knee beside Treat's rocker. "Treat Dandridge, will you marry me?" she asked with a hitch in her breath.

Treat was surprised. She thought she'd be the one asking Mickey to marry her. A laugh bubbled out of her unbidden.

"Anywhere, anytime, Mickey Heiden. You have only to name the time and the place, and Bella and I will be there with bells on."

About the Author

Kay Bigelow was born in Alabama and three months later began her world travels. She has lived in Germany, Italy, Hong Kong, and much of the U.S. Her novels and short stories are often set in the various places she has lived. She has finally settled down (for the time being) in a small town in northern Washington State.

Books Available From Bold Strokes Books

A Date to Die by Anne Laughlin. Someone is killing people close to Detective Kay Adler, who must look to her own troubled past for a suspect. There she finds more than one person seeking revenge against her. (978-163555-023-8)

Captured Soul by Laydin Michaels. Can Kadence Munroe save the woman she loves from a twisted killer, or will she lose her to a collector of souls? (978-162639-915-0)

Dawn's New Day by TJ Thomas. Can Dawn Oliver and Cam Cooper, two women who have loved and lost, open their hearts to love again? (978-163555-072-6)

Definite Possibility by Maggie Cummings. Sam Miller is just out for good times, but Lucy Weston makes her realize happily ever after is a definite possibility. (978-162639-909-9)

Eyes Like Those by Melissa Brayden. Isabel Chase and Taylor Andrews struggle between love and ambition from the writers' room on one of Hollywood's hottest TV shows. (978-163555-012-2)

Heart's Orders by Jaycie Morrison. Helen Tucker and Tee Owens escape hardscrabble lives to careers in the Women's Army Corps, but more than their hearts are at risk as friendship blossoms into love. (978-163555-073-3)

Hiding Out by Kay Bigelow. Treat Dandridge is unaware that her life is in danger from the murderer who is hunting the woman she's falling in love with, Mickey Heiden. (978-162639-983-9)

Omnipotence Enough by Sophia Kell Hagin. Can the tiny tool that abducted war veteran Jamie Gwynmorgan accidentally acquires help her escape an unknown enemy to reclaim her stolen life and the woman she deeply loves? (978-163555-037-5)

Summer's Cove by Aurora Rey. Emerson Lange moved to Provincetown to live in the moment, but when she meets Darcy Belo and her son Liam, her quest for summer romance becomes a family affair. (978-162639-971-6)

The Road to Wings by Julie Tizard. Lieutenant Casey Tompkins, Air Force student pilot, has to fly with the toughest instructor, Captain Kathryn "Hard Ass" Hardesty, fly a supersonic jet, and deal with a growing forbidden attraction. (978-162639-988-4)

Beauty and the Boss by Ali Vali. Ellis Renois is at the top of the fashion world, but she never expects her summer assistant Charlotte Hamner to tear her heart and her business apart like sharp scissors through cheap material. (978-162639-919-8)

Fury's Choice by Brey Willows. When gods walk amongst humans, can two women find a balance between love and faith? (978-162639-869-6)

Lessons in Desire by MJ Williamz. Can a summer love stand a four-month hiatus and still burn hot? (978-163555-019-1)

Lightning Chasers by Cass Sellars. For Sydney and Parker, being a couple was never what they had planned. Now they have to fight corruption, murder, and enemies hiding in plain sight just to hold on to each other. Lightning Series, Book Two. (978-162639-965-5)

Summer Fling by Jean Copeland. Still jaded from a breakup years earlier, Kate struggles to trust falling in love again when a summer fling with sexy young singer Jordan rocks her off her feet. (978-162639-981-5)

Take Me There by Julie Cannon. Adrienne and Sloan know it would be career suicide to mix business with pleasure, however tempting it is. But what's the harm? They're both consenting adults. Who would know? (978-162639-917-4)

Unchained Memories by Dena Blake. Can a woman give herself completely when she's left a piece of herself behind? (978-162639-993-8)

Walking Through Shadows by Sheri Lewis Wohl. All Molly wanted to do was go backpacking…in her own century. (978-162639-968-6)

Freedom to Love by Ronica Black. What happens when the woman who spent her life worrying about caring for her family finally finds the freedom to love without borders? (978-1-63555-001-6)

A Lamentation of Swans by Valerie Bronwen. Ariel Montgomery returns to Sea Oats to try to save her broken marriage but soon finds herself also fighting to save her own life and catch a murderer. (978-1-62639-828-3)

House of Fate by Barbara Ann Wright. Two women must throw off the lives they've known as a guardian and an assassin and save two rival houses before their secrets tear the galaxy apart. (978-1-62639-780-4)

Planning for Love by Erin Dutton. Could true love be the one thing that wedding coordinator Faith McKenna didn't plan for? (978-1-62639-954-9)

Sidebar by Carsen Taite. Judge Camille Avery and her clerk, attorney West Fallon, agree on little except their mutual attraction, but can their relationship and their careers survive a headline-grabbing case? (978-1-62639-752-1)

Sweet Boy and Wild One by T. L. Hayes. When Rachel Cole meets soulful singer Bobby Layton at an open mic, she is immediately in thrall. What she soon discovers will rock her world in ways she never imagined. (978-1-62639-963-1)

To Be Determined by Mardi Alexander and Laurie Eichler. Charlie Dickerson escapes her life in the US to rescue Australian wildlife with Pip Atkins, but can they save each other? (978-1-62639-946-4)

True Colors by Yolanda Wallace. Blogger Robby Rawlins plans to use First Daughter Taylor Crenshaw to get ahead, but she never planned on falling in love with her in the process. (978-1-62639-927-3)

Heart Stop by Radclyffe. Two women, one with a damaged body, the other a damaged spirit, challenge each other to dare to live again. (978-1-62639-899-3)

Undercover Affairs by Julie Blair. Searching for stolen documents crucial to U.S. security, CIA agent Rett Spenser confronts lies, deceit, and unexpected romance as she investigates art gallery owner Shannon Kent. (978-1-62639-905-1)

Taking Sides by Kathleen Knowles. When passion and politics collide, can love survive? (978-1-62639-876-4)

Unexpected by Jenny Frame. When Dale McGuire falls for Rebecca Harper, the mother of the son she never knew she had, will Rebecca's troubled past stop them from making the family they both truly crave? (978-1-62639-942-6)

Canvas for Love by Charlotte Greene. When ghosts from Amelia's past threaten to undermine their relationship, Chloé must navigate the greatest romance of her life without losing sight of who she is. (978-1-62639-944-0)

Repercussions by Jessica L. Webb. Someone planted information in Edie Black's brain and now they want it back, but with the protection of shy former soldier Skye Kenny, Edie has a chance at life and love. (978-1-62639-925-9)

Spark by Catherine Friend. Jamie's life is turned upside down when her consciousness travels back to 1560 and lands in the body of one of Queen Elizabeth I's ladies-in-waiting…or has she totally lost her grip on reality? (978-1-62639-930-3)

Thorns of the Past by Gun Brooke. Former cop Darcy Flynn's heart broke when her career on the force ended in disgrace, but perhaps saving Sabrina Hawk's life will mend it in more ways than one. (978-1-62639-857-3)

You Make Me Tremble by Karis Walsh. Seismologist Casey Radnor comes to the San Juan Islands to study an earthquake but finds her heart shaken by passion when she meets animal rescuer Iris Mallery. (978-1-62639-901-3)

Girls Next Door, edited by Sandy Lowe and Stacia Seaman. Best-selling romance authors tell it from the heart—sexy, romantic stories of falling for the girls next door. (978-1-62639-916-7)

Complications by MJ Williamz. Two women battle for the heart of one. (978-1-62639-769-9)

Crossing the Wide Forever by Missouri Vaun. As Cody Walsh and Lillie Ellis face the perils of the untamed West, they discover that love's uncharted frontier isn't for the weak in spirit or the faint of heart. (978-1-62639-851-1)

boldstrokesbooks.com

Bold Strokes Books

Quality and Diversity in LGBTQ Literature

 victory EDITIONS

 Drama

 MATINEE BOOKS

SCI-FI

E-BOOKS

MYSTERY

 erotica

EROTICA

 SOLILOQUY

 BOLD STROKES BOOKS

YOUNG ADULT

 LIBERTY EDITIONS

Romance

W·E·B·S·T·O·R·E

PRINT AND EBOOKS